A
HIGHLAND
Heist

A CONTEMPORARY HIGHLAND ROMANCE
BOOK THREE

CALI MACKAY

A Highland Heist
by Cali MacKay
Copyright © 2012 by Cali MacKay
Published by Cali MacKay
http://calimackay.com

Printed in the United States of America
First Printing, 2012, first edition
ISBN: 978-1-940041-10-0

Contents

For Joe, Maeve and Amelia.

CHAPTER
One

ON ALL FOURS, Maggie ignored the footsteps coming up behind her, with no more than a fleeting thought to her rear end, which was sticking up high in the air as she struggled with a stubborn bolt, the front half of her body wedged behind the wood paneling. Her fingers cramped as she felt around to try to loosen the connection, working blind in the near dark of the enclosure. Nearly there…and then the last of the stuck bolts twisted free. She finished and pulled herself out of the opening in the wall, only to find her new client standing there with another man at his side.

Perfect. She hauled herself to her feet and dusted her hands off on the legs of her jeans, trying to ignore the raised eyebrows on her client and the analytical look of the stranger, whose eyes drifted past her face to somewhere just above her head. Casually, she reached up and tried to smooth her hair. Uncontrollable to begin with, it seemed to have picked up a miscellany of cobwebs and dust. She managed to keep her groan from escaping. Nice first impression.

Iain MacCraigh's lips quirked into an amused smile. "I'm sorry to be bothering ye when ye're working, but I wanted to introduce ye to Conall Stewart. He's in charge of computer security for all my businesses and home, so ye'll need to integrate the work ye'll be doing here on the museum with his existing systems."

So, this was the computer genius Iain had mentioned. She wasn't sure how she felt about having a stranger involved in her project, but at least he was good—really good. Not one to leave things to chance when it came to her work, she'd researched Conall thoroughly after Iain first told her they'd be working together, and she was impressed. Not an easy thing to do.

She considered herself to be at the top in her field, and if she was going to be stuck working with him, then at least he knew what he was doing. As a woman in the male-dominated field of high-end security, she was damned if she'd have her hard-earned reputation damaged by working with someone who wasn't up to snuff. And she sure as hell wouldn't risk the Highlander's Hope, a treasure of priceless value. The system she was putting in for the museum Iain was building would incorporate her most advanced designs and equipment.

With a smile, Maggie shook Conall's hand as she took him in, her gaze wandering over his handsome form. There was certainly something about the man that had her pulse kicking. "It's a pleasure."

His hair was just long and wavy enough to have a mind of its own, the color of it like honey and aged whisky. Yet it was his eyes that held her attention—a warm amber flecked with gold and chocolate, lit from within with a fire and intelligence. He was tall and well-built for someone who sat at a computer all day, and his scruffy stubble made her want to reach out and run her fingers across his strong jawline.

This could be fun—except for the fact that the man looked far too serious for his own good. With luck, she'd get him to pull the stick out of his arse. Life was too short to not take full advantage of all it had to offer—a lesson she'd learned the hard way.

Conall mumbled a half-hearted greeting in response, before giving Iain a quick glance. "I'd like to get started if ye don't mind. There's a lot to be done, especially if we're to have everything ready and in place for the New Year's ribbon cutting."

Iain turned to her with a consoling smile, his eyebrows flicking up in a way that said *better you than me*. "Well then…I'll not delay ye any further. If ye need me for anything, I'll be back at the house. Cat will be back later this afternoon, so don't be too surprised if ye find her snooping around. Good day to the both of ye."

Once Iain had gone, Conall stood there, his eyes locked on hers. "Maggie Brennan, aye? Twenty-seven. Head of Brennan Securities out of Dublin, Ireland. Co-founded with yer father, Liam Brennan, though he acts as more of a consultant. Ye graduated top of yer class from Trinity at the early age of eighteen, and have won several awards for yer innovative designs and inventions. Three younger brothers, one who works for ye. Unmarried, no children. And ye drive a motorcycle—far too fast, if yer speeding tickets are anything to go by."

She crossed her arms in front of her chest, pinning him with an unwavering gaze, amusement fighting with the slight annoyance that wanted to rear its ugly head. So the boy had done his homework. Fair enough. But she was no gombeen.

Her lips tugged into a hint of a smile. "Conall Stewart…Twenty-eight. Founder and sole employee of Stewart Technologies. Graduated from MIT before returning back home to Dunmuir, Scotland, where you were born and raised. Your specialty is hacking into company networks to find their vulnerabilities so you can then reinforce their systems. Never been married, and ye have no sprogs. Parents are divorced, one younger sister. Ye live alone in a home you own outright, and ye drive your Audi far too slow—if your lack of speeding tickets are anything to go by."

"Hmph." He looked her over for what felt like a very long time, but she held her ground and his gaze. When he spoke, it was still with no humor, as if he was tolerating her because he had no choice. "Might as well get started then."

By the gods, serious as he was, she was going to love pushing his buttons. She grabbed her bag of tools and headed across the room, leaving him to follow as he would. She glanced over at him, a smile breaking through to the surface, unable to remain serious for long.

"So do ye always look like ye swallowed sour milk or is the pleasure all mine?" That got her a glare, and she had to laugh. "I'm just yanking your tail. Curious to see what ye might look like if ye actually smiled a bit. Bet you'd be handsome. Or are ye worried 'bout the wrinkles? They've got creams for that, ye know."

His mouth pursed into a thin line. "I'm here to work, aye? Not to socialize. So if ye don't mind…"

Her anger sparked and bristled just below the surface as she stopped and pinned him with an icy stare. Reminding herself that she'd be working with Conall for the foreseeable future, she bit back the sarcastic remarks that wanted to spew forth, and told herself to let it go, knowing she was overreacting.

She took a deep breath and forced herself to calm down a notch or two, though when she spoke it was through gritted teeth. "Just so we're clear—*nothing* gets in the way of my work. Nothing. Don't take my humor and amiable mood for disinterest or incompetence. It'll be a mistake you'll regret."

Was it…could it be? Her eyes must be deceiving her. A smile tugged at his lips. "I've no doubt ye could make me regret many a thing, lass. Now if we could get back to work—please—I'd greatly appreciate it."

If she were being generous, she might even take that as a sort of apology. She grinned, her anger dissipating and her humor back. "Happy to oblige ye."

As they moved through the construction area, Maggie looked around at the progress being made. Though she was there to tackle the technical end of the security system for the museum, the bulk of the project fell to the construction crew who'd be transforming the old church ruins on the MacCraigh land, and rebuilding them into a museum that would house the Highlander's Hope and the paintings that had supplied the clues that enabled Cat and Iain to find the bejeweled necklace. There would be additional space reserved for items Cat planned to get on loan from other museums.

With the structural parts of the museum built, she and her brother were laying the foundation and wiring for the systems and tech they'd soon be installing. "With the electrical now in, we've run the cables that will support the final safeguards and security measures. We're using the most current tech so that any disturbances to the system will be detected—whether physical or over the Net. If ye have changes you want made to the computer securities, I'm happy to work with ye so the systems run seamlessly."

Conall wandered, stepping over construction debris and tools, as his gaze took it all in. "I'll need to see yer security schematics and blueprints. Depending on how ye've set it up, there may need to be some changes made."

She sighed. This was why she hated having others work on her projects. As a security company, they were more than capable of handling the computer end of things, even if her specialty was creating security tech—complicated biometrics, motion and interference detectors, photoelectric scanners, and anything else her mind could dream up.

At least Conall was one of the best in his field. It only made sense that he'd want to look things over. He wasn't passing judgment on her work, but rather making sure everything operated at an optimal level.

She stepped to his side and looked up at him, liking how the sun streamed through the tall windows and gilded him in gold. "They're in my work trailer. If ye'd like to join me, we can go over them there. Or I could drop them off at your office."

"I work from home." He gave her his business card. "I'd like to see them now, but if you could also get me my own copy, it'd be much appreciated."

"I'll drop one off for ye later." She tilted her head with a smile. "In the meantime, follow me. My bus is out the back."

She led him outdoors to the RV she used when working away from home. It housed all her supplies and tools, and acted as a workshop, allowing her to make adjustments to her gear and tech without having to leave the worksite. She'd had it custom made to her specifications, and then outfitted it further with her own tech. The vehicle itself had cost her a pretty penny, but it was a necessity when she was constantly away from home. It offered her a bit of familiarity and comfort in her ever-changing environment.

Letting them in past the safeguards, she climbed up the steps with Conall trailing right behind her. Though large and spacious for a bus, it was packed with equipment, forcing them to squeeze through towards the back where she kept all her plans and diagrams. There'd been larger models to choose from, but she hadn't wanted to run into problems while travelling down the tight, winding roads once outside the city. "Ye'll have to excuse the tight quarters. I think I overpacked for the job. Didn't want to need something and not have it."

With eyebrows raised, he glanced around, though his expression had yet to change much. "Do ye also sleep here?"

She could have laughed at the way he was eyeballing the place. It was clear he didn't care for the cramped accommodations. "I have in the past, but with this job scheduled to last months, I've opted to rent a place not far from here."

Paging through her blueprints, she pulled out the ones she needed and handed them to Conall. He laid them out on the table and took a quick look. "Do ye mind if I take these back to the museum?"

"Not at all. Just make sure I get them back before ye go, and I'd greatly appreciate it if ye don't leave them lying around—or show them to anyone, for that matter." He probably thought she was being paranoid, but she didn't care. She took plenty of risks in life—just not with her work.

His eyes narrowed with a glare. "Ye're not the only professional here, lass."

She beamed at him with a big smile, refusing to get into a pissing match. "Well, I'm glad to hear it. As soon as I dig out the blueprint printer, I'll get ye your own copy of the schematics and drop them off. Now if ye don't mind, get out. I've got work to do."

His lips quirked into a smile. "Ye know, we may just get along after all."

CHAPTER Two

Bloody hell…what time was it? And who the hell was pounding on his door so early in the morning and getting his crazy dog riled up? Conall dragged his alarm clock over. Six twelve. He groaned and rolled out of bed, ready to murder whoever had woken him up.

He threw on some pajama bottoms, after quickly debating whether to just head down there naked—and it'd serve them right. Padding down the stairs, he nearly tripped on Piper, who was still barking and clearly determined to get tangled between his legs.

Grabbing Piper by the collar to prevent her from escaping yet again, he yanked the door open, his words already spewing forth amid his curses. "What the…"

He groaned. Maggie. It figured.

"Did I wake ye? Had your plans and didn't want to hold up your work, in case ye were an early riser—which I see that ye're not—and figured while I was at it, I'd go for a quick run. Want to join me? Nothing like a morning run to get the blood flowing first thing when ye wake. There are other options, of course, but… a run was easier this morning." She looked up at him, finally, blessedly, quiet. How many coffees did the woman already have?

"Go away." He spun and slammed the door, only to hear knocking again. He yanked it open. "Woman, I'm ready to murder ye."

She just smiled. Infuriatingly, smugly smiled. Not a care in the world. "Well, you could at least take the plans. And I'll assume it's a *no* on going for a run? Do ye want me to take your dog instead? Looks like she'd enjoy it—might get rid of some of her energy."

He grabbed the leash he kept by the door, quickly clipped it to the squirming pup's collar and shoved the handle at Maggie, grabbing the plans. "Her name's Piper. Don't fall off the cliff."

The second his crazy mutt took off—which took all of a nanosecond—he slammed the door once more, and crawled back to bed.

Except that his sleep was now ruined. After tossing and turning, sleep refusing to return, he dragged himself back out of bed. Grumbling and cursing, he put on a pot of coffee and while waiting for it to brew, booted up his laptop. He logged in to work and checked his email. Once he ensured there wasn't anything that needed his immediate attention, he pulled out the schematics Maggie left for him.

One map after another, layer upon layer of security. It was clear the lass left nothing to chance, even backing up her back-up plans. He supposed that's what happened when someone was not only thorough, but hyper. Bloody hell, the woman must inject the caffeine directly into her vein. Six twelve. And looking fresh as a spring morning, a blush on her cheeks and a sparkle in her glacier-blue eyes.

He took a closer look and worked through her diagrams. Maybe…It'd be hard to improve the securities and firewalls she'd put in place—and frankly, that wasn't his job—but he could possibly make things a bit more efficient and speed up response.

It'd be easy enough to integrate her systems for the Hope with the ones he already had in place on Iain's mainframe for his other businesses. Opening a new document, he started making notes on the changes he'd like to address. That would be an interesting meeting, for he was sure her back would immediately go up before she wrangled her temper under control. At least it seemed short lived, flaring into life for just a moment, before sense and reasoning pushed it aside, and she was back to her perky, smiley self.

It was clear Maggie liked to be in control, especially when it came to her work, and that was definitely something he understood. When you worked hard to build a reputation, you couldn't let others ruin it. But if she thought he'd step to the side and let her stomp all over his turf, then she was gravely mistaken. They'd just have to do their best to work together, especially since they were stuck with each other for the next few months.

He checked the time. Maggie had been gone a while—close to an hour and a half. Was that normal for one of her runs? Or had Piper dragged her off the cliff and into the raging sea and jagged rocks below? He groaned and got back to work, doing his best to ignore the feeling of impending doom.

A few more notes—and he checked the time again. Damn it. He'd give her another ten minutes. Yet, looking back at the schematics, he found his concentration was shattered, his gaze drifting to check the time yet again.

Cursing, he set aside his laptop and got to his feet, knowing he'd not forgive himself if something happened to her while he did nothing but sit on the sofa. He got on his hiking boots and grabbed a sweater just as there was a knock at his door.

Relief washed over him, though he was ready to give her a tongue-lashing for making him worry. Grinding his teeth, he got a hold of himself and pushed his annoyance to the side, knowing it was his own fault for giving a rat's arse.

He pulled open the door and watched her breeze in, dragging his pup behind her. "What the hell happened to her?"

She looked down at the dog before turning those blue eyes on him with a look of confusion, a smile tugging at her full lips. "I took her for a run. How is she supposed to look?"

"That dog's crazy—and hasn't ever stopped being crazy. I've never seen her this—"

"Calm?" Her eyebrows perked in question as her smile widened.

"Aye. Calm." A deep blush stood out against her luminous skin, her cheeks flushed from the exertion of her run and the brisk wind from the sea.

"It's amazing what a bit of a workout can do for the mind and body." She reached down and unclipped the leash before handing it to him. "I can come by and get her again tomorrow if ye'd like. I hadn't realized it when ye gave me your card, not being familiar with the roads and all, but we're neighbors."

He squeezed his eyes shut for a long moment, his head suddenly pounding. "Och, tell me ye're not staying at the Campbell cottage." Rowan Campbell had moved in with her boyfriend, Angus Macleod, a few months ago, leaving the home empty.

"That's the one. Belongs to a friend of Iain's. They were happy to rent it to me since it was just sitting there, and it's got two rooms, which is convenient since my brother will be joining me for this job sometime in the upcoming weeks—had a bit of an overlap in projects."

It figured, since Iain and Angus were the best of friends. And if Maggie was in the Campbell cottage, that made her his closest neighbor. Shite.

"No need to take the dog for a run tomorrow—or any other day for that matter." He'd never get to sleep in if she kept coming around to steal Piper.

"Ah…well then, I'll leave it as an open offer in case ye change your mind." She started to wander, her gaze drifting around the room. "Mind if I grab a drink?"

"This way." He sighed. At least she seemed to have mellowed out a bit. Only took her over an hour of exercise. "Since I couldn't get back to sleep after being dragged out of my bed at the bloody crack of dawn, I got started on the schematics."

She followed him into the kitchen, beaming a huge smile at him. "See! You got a head start on yer day. Doesn't that make ye feel good?"

"*No.*" He pinned her with a steely gaze, hoping she'd get it through that pretty head of hers and leave him alone. "I get plenty done on my own schedule, thank ye very much."

Her brows perked up in mock defense. "Never said ye didn't, boyo. Don't go getting yer knickers in a twist."

He grabbed a glass, tossed some ice in it and filled it with water. "Here."

"Thanks." She drank half of it in one go. "So do ye want to go over the changes? Or are ye kicking me out?"

Damn if he wasn't tempted—just to make his point. Yet he didn't show her the door—and she would no doubt make him regret his decision. "Might as well get started since ye're already here."

He led them into his living room where he liked to work. She wandered about, taking it all in. "This is *really* nice. Wow."

"Thanks." Though she was right—it was a gorgeous room—he was pleased that she liked it. He'd renovated the older home a few years back and the living room was his favorite, with a large stone fireplace that ran up to a cathedral ceiling and a row of windows flanking it, opening the room to the cliffs and sea just beyond.

"Ooo…do ye play?" She'd wandered over to where his guitar sat in the corner, unused for far too long.

His back went up as he pushed back the wave of emotions that hit him, and tried not to speak through gritted teeth. "No. Not anymore. If we could get to work…?"

Her eyebrows perked in question, but she said no more as they took a seat on the sofa, side by side, where he'd been working.

He unplugged his laptop and handed it to her, ignoring the way his shoulder and thigh brushed against hers as he shifted towards her to point to the diagram he'd pulled up on the screen. "The schematics ye've drawn up are great, but ye'll see I've made some changes to the routing, which will make things more efficient and speed up yer processes."

With her brow furrowed and her lips pressed together, she looked over his proposed changes. He was half expecting her to refuse to make the adjustments or give him a tongue-lashing for messing with her work and plans. Instead she continued to read on, her gaze intense.

She looked over and nodded, a smile slowly turning up on those full lips. "Nice work, Conall. I think ye'll be a good addition to the project."

Oh. Not quite what he'd expected. It's not that he needed her approval, but it was nice to know the next few months of working with her might be amicable. "Well, I appreciate ye saying so."

She handed him back the laptop, her blue eyes alight. "I should get going. Still need to shower before heading to the job site."

He stood with her and walked her to the door. "I'll see ye there, aye?"

She nodded and walked off, the cottage only a quarter of a mile down the road. He watched her go, her thick hair pulling free of its bindings as the wind blew in off the sea. She could be a dangerous distraction— except that he had no time for distractions of that sort. Nor did he have the desire.

Yet he still stood there, watching.

CHAPTER Three

H APPY WITH EVERYTHING she'd managed to accomplish, Maggie decided to wrap things up for the day. She'd seen Conall poking around while working on his own things, but they'd both been busy. There was something about him that she found intriguing. It was as if he gave off a certain energy which immediately pulled her into his orbit and she couldn't help but be drawn to him. She knew it the moment he walked into a room, the air around her shifting with his presence, making her fully aware of the nearness of him.

Maybe it had to do with his sharp intelligence—or how stern and serious he was. Not many seemed to challenge him or get in his way, not wanting to be on the receiving end of one of those golden glares. Not that it bothered her any. It only made her curious to find out what was behind the façade—and she had no doubt it could be a whole lot of fun finding out. Alone on the job site, Conall could be just the thing she needed to keep boredom at bay when she wasn't working.

That was one of the advantages to working with her brother, Liam. They got along well, and when working in an area when they knew not a soul, it was good to have his company—when he was around. In the meantime, she'd have to find other ways to keep herself entertained, and for now that plan included Conall, even if he didn't know it yet.

Andrew wandered towards her as she packed up her tools. He was the foreman for the construction company that was rebuilding the church ruins, and definitely a good-looking man. From London, he was in his late twenties or early thirties, tall with a muscular build, sable brown hair and brown eyes. He seemed nice, and normally she'd be more than a little interested. Yet she just couldn't get into him for some reason. Their chemistry seemed off. Not that he had given up trying.

"I don't suppose I could interest you in a bite to eat and a pint. The pub has surprisingly good food, and seeing how it's a Friday, I was thinking we could venture towards one of the larger towns not too far from here. If you're up for it, of course." Andrew hitched a thumb in his jean pocket, his head cocked to one side, a lazy smile on his lips.

She zipped her bag and stood. "I appreciate the offer, but I have to catch up on some emails and other work."

"Are you sure? I promise to keep you entertained—and it's not like the emails won't be there when you get back. Come on, Maggie. You'll have the whole weekend to answer them, and you've got to eat at some point, right?" He shifted his weight as his gaze wandered over her face, a sweet smile on his lips.

Iain walked over and saved her from having to come up with another excuse. "I'm glad I caught ye before ye'd left for the day. If ye have no plans for the evening, Cat would love to have everyone over for dinner—wants to thank ye all for the hard work ye've been putting in. Not to mention, she's been experimenting with some new recipe and is desperate for mouths to feed."

Not exactly what Maggie had planned for the evening, but she knew better than to turn down invitations from her clients, especially when they were wealthy and well-connected. She glanced at Andrew, wondering if she'd be stuck turning down his advances the rest of the night. Probably no way to avoid it.

She managed a smile for Iain and hefted her bag onto her shoulder. "Sure. Thanks for the invite."

Andrew smiled in her direction before looking back to Iain. "Sounds perfect to me."

Iain clapped his hands together. "Excellent. If seven works for ye, that would be grand."

Maggie hefted her tool bag onto her shoulder and followed him towards the door, hoping to leave Andrew behind. Luckily, it worked. "I'll see you then."

With her tools locked up on the bus and everything secured for the night, she grabbed her helmet and hopped on her motorbike, a gorgeous Triumph Speedmaster. Black, moody, and mean, she loved her bike. Loved the feel of its rumble and speed.

"Ye heading home?" It was a Scottish lilt rather than Andrew's English.

Relieved, she turned to find Conall walking towards her, his car parked next to her bike in the makeshift parking lot. It was currently no more than grass, dirt, and puddles of mud, but it'd all get paved over once the construction wrapped up. "Yeah. I'm desperate to get home and wash the day's dirt and grime off me. The beginning of a job is always the dirtiest."

The old church had most of its walls standing before the renovation started, but the roof had been mostly caved in. Cat and Iain had spared little expense adding on to it and bringing the original part of the building back to life. It'd be gorgeous once it was completed, a perfect home for the Hope.

"I wanted to thank ye for taking Piper on that run. She was knackered afterwards. Never seen her so quiet in all my life." He shifted his weight, repositioning the strap of his laptop bag.

If Maggie had to guess, this was probably the longest conversation the man had all month outside of work. "Like I said, I'm happy to take her with me in the mornings. She's good company."

He barked out a laugh. "Is she now?"

Maggie shrugged, a smile tugging at her lips. "Well, a running partner who actually speaks would also be nice. But since I know I've got a better chance of getting hell to freeze over than to get ye out for a run with me, Piper will have to do."

"I run. On occasion." His eyes narrowed in annoyance as the wind caught his hair, blowing it across his face.

"Do ye now? Well then, I might just have to drag ye with me." She could have laughed at the expression on his face. "Or not. I'm happy to change up my exercise routine if there's something else ye'd rather do."

She could think of *so* many different ways to get a workout with him. She just couldn't help herself. A woman would have to be blind to miss that the man was damn good looking with his strong jaw covered in stubble not quite long enough to be a beard, thick longish hair, and those gold eyes, so incredibly cat-like. Damn. He made her want to be so very bad—not at all professional of her, even if she didn't mind crossing that line once she'd clocked off for the day.

"Did Iain invite ye to dinner?" He shifted his weight again, as if growing impatient.

"He did—and Andrew too. I take it yer going?" It'd be nice to have someone other than Andrew and her employers there.

Not that she didn't like Cat and Iain. They were great—but they were still her clients. And the last thing she wanted or needed was to be encouraging Andrew by hanging around with him. She liked him enough and on paper he looked great, but that spark between them was missing, and there was nothing you could really do about that sort of thing.

A hint of a smile tugged at his lips, transforming his face and lighting his eyes with a fire she hadn't expected. "A bit hard to say no, isn't it? Don't get me wrong—they're great. But it's not really my thing."

She met his smile with a wider one of her own. "I had the same exact thought. Guess I'll see ye later then?"

"Aye. I suppose so."

She kicked her bike to life, the roar of it breaking the silence of the glen. With a grin at Conall and a teasing flick of her eyebrows, she put on her helmet and took off, knowing he was still watching her—and no doubt thinking she was going too fast. She had to laugh. Fast indeed. The bike hugged the curves of the winding roads, as the engine thrummed underneath her, her ride home already over just as she was starting to really enjoy herself.

With more than two hours to get ready for dinner, Maggie opted for a nice long soak in the tub, her mind wandering to the things she'd need to accomplish in the next few days. Once she started a project, she always liked to rethink things. It was one thing to design a system based on the diagrams you'd been given, and another to actually see the space you'd be working with—especially once you had the chance to work the area and become familiar with the space and its quirks. And old places had quirks aplenty.

The changes Conall wanted to make were good ones, and she found that she didn't mind working with him. They seemed to respect each other's work territory, and that wasn't something she always got on a job site.

It left her wondering what Conall would be like tonight. Would he remain serious and tight-lipped? Or would he relax a bit once he wasn't working? She'd caught glimpses of what he might be like if he'd just loosen up—and she'd be happy to help him get there, even if she had to drag him, kicking and screaming. He was a challenge, and one she'd be happy to tackle.

Knowing she'd have to ride her bike to Iain's, she picked out a pair of dark skinny jeans and a pretty bohemian top, and then paired it with her leather jacket and calf-hugging chocolate suede boots as she headed out the door, a bottle of wine in hand. Again, the ride to Cat and Iain's was a short one, and she swore she'd take the weekend to go for a nice long ride along the coast.

Cat answered the door and invited her in, taking her jacket and the bottle of wine with a thank-you. "I'm so glad you could make it. Everyone's hanging around by the fire, and be sure to get Angus to pour you a drink. I just have a few last-minute things to take care of, but I hope you'll make yourself at home."

Maggie let Cat get back to her cooking as she looked around the place on her way to the sitting room. She remembered the small castle from her first visit to meet with Cat and Iain, and found that she was still as captivated by the place as she was the first time around. The tall ceilings, the aged dark wood paneling, the ancient tapestries, the period paintings—and a far too inadequate security system. She'd have to mention it to them in the near future.

She quickly scanned the room of people, realizing she knew almost everyone there. Angus and Rowan, whom she'd met when she rented the cottage from them, and there was Andrew and his boss, Phillip, along with a few more of their employees, Johnny and Clyde. There was an older gentleman, whom she believed to be Iain's father, and Cat's assistant, Tansy. Conall had yet to show up or was wandering about elsewhere in the home. Not that Maggie was disappointed—not yet, at least.

Andrew spotted her, but she avoided his gaze and wandered towards the bar, happy to make small talk with her landlords. In response to Angus's question, she said, "A glass of red would be lovely. Thanks."

"How's the cottage working out?" Rowan cringed with a smile. "I know it's pretty basic—and it can get damn cold and drafty."

"Actually, it's perfect. It's big enough, everything works, and the views are just gorgeous. The area's perfect for a morning run." Though she might sleep in tomorrow morning.

Angus's brow furrowed. "I hope ye'll be careful, lass. It gets foggy in the morning and ye don't want to stumble off the cliff."

She gave him a smile. "That's what Conall said—though with fewer words."

Rowan laughed. "Sounds about right. Isn't he also working on the museum?"

"He is. In fact, we'll be working together so my systems work seamlessly with his. I'm surprised he's not here already." She glanced over her shoulder, but he still wasn't around—and she'd now inadvertently caught Andrew's attention. Turning back to her discussion, she hoped she could avoid him just a little longer.

Angus scoffed. "I'm not in the least bit surprised. Probably waiting until the last moment to show. Hell, I'm shocked he even agreed to come. He's yer neighbor, ye know."

Humor sparked in Angus's eyes, making Maggie think he was far too mischievous a man. He threw Rowan a glance that spoke volumes—one of those looks between lovers when they need no words. She missed that silent communication. The way you could have an entire conversation with a simple look. And Angus was clearly head over heels in love with the beautiful redhead.

It made her think of her own love life—or lack thereof. It was hard when she was constantly on the road. Eventually she'd like to give a serious relationship another try, though she'd learned from her past mistakes. It was one thing to have a bit of casual fun, but if she were going to fall in love and give her heart to another, she could only do that utterly and completely—and they better be willing to do the same. She refused to settle for someone who couldn't reciprocate at the same level.

Thinking of Angus's words and her morning run, she had to smile. "I actually paid him a visit this morning to drop off some plans and see if he wanted to go for a run, but I'm afraid I probably woke him up. He's got a great dog, though. Ended up taking her with me."

A smile danced on Rowan's lips, her eyes sparkling. "Be forewarned—Piper's a bit of an escape artist. Although she's gotten into the habit of beelining it to the cottage when she does get loose."

Angus shook his head, his lips pursed, though there was still humor in his eyes. "That's because ye'd give her treats when she showed up at yer door. It's no wonder she tries to escape every chance she gets. Rewarding bad behavior is a very bad habit, love."

Rowan laughed. "Don't go blaming me. I'm not the one letting her escape. And at least this way, Conall knows where to find her."

Angus tilted his head. "Speak of the devil."

Conall approached while scanning the room, his brow furrowed. Maggie had to wonder if it was permanent, though there was no doubt having to come to dinner with a large crowd wasn't helping his mood. He looked like the type to avoid socializing at all cost. "Hey."

"A man of many words." Rowan teased Conall with a smile jumping to her lips as he glared at her.

"No point in yammering." He flicked a glance in Maggie's direction as if accusing her of just that.

Maggie barked out a laugh. "That would be me then, aye? Yeah, I know I seldom shut me gob, but that's because I like ye. If I ever stop talking, that's when ye know you're in trouble and need to worry. Won't say I don't have a wee bit of a temper, but at least I'll warn ye."

It was almost as if he were fighting to hold back the hint of a smile that seemed to tug at his lips. "Lucky me."

"Damn right—and don't ye be forgetting it either." Her eyes narrowed to a stare, though she hoped he saw the humor there.

Rowan's smile widened as she gave Conall a look, while linking her arm with Angus's. "We should go check in on Cat and Iain. If you'll excuse us."

"I like them—they're good together." Maggie watched them go; though having played match-maker herself on more than one occasion, she suspected their departure was a ploy to leave her and Conall alone together. Not that it was going to happen. Andrew approached, and there was no way to escape without being rude.

"You look lovely tonight, Maggie." Andrew all but ignored Conall, his gaze focused on her.

"Thanks. Have ye met?" She linked a hand around Conall's arm, flicking him a silent plea with her eyes. Maybe Andrew would let up if he thought she was dating someone. "Conall, this is Andrew. Andrew, Conall."

"The computer guy, right?" Andrew looked from her to Conall, and then, as if dismissing Conall as not being a worthy rival, refocused his attention back on Maggie—not that Conall was one to be easily dismissed.

"Aye, the computer guy. And…I'm sorry, I'm not familiar with what it is ye do." Conall covered her hand with his, his gaze landing casually on Andrew, as if he were of no real consequence—and certainly no threat.

He pinned Conall with a look of annoyance. "I'm the foreman. I'm running the project."

"The construction end, aye? Wouldn't know much about that part of the project, I'm afraid. Security is my specialty—just like Maggie here. Speaking of which…" He gave her a rare smile. "I'd like to discuss those plans if ye have a moment."

"That would be perfect—I've been meaning to speak to ye about that." She turned back to Andrew. "If ye'll excuse us."

Conall escorted her away from Andrew and to a more private part of the room, not far from the fireplace. Once they were alone, he let her arm slip free and turned to face her, his voice kept low. "Do ye want to tell me what the hell that was about?"

Her shoulders slumped as she let out a deep breath. "It's nothing really. He's been lingering and trying to get friendly, and doesn't seem to get that I'm not interested. I'm sorry that I grabbed your arm to keep him at bay."

"Well, I'm not sure he'll be leaving ye alone now that ye've made it a competition between us." He ran a rough hand through his hair and shook his head. "I don't need this sort of complication, Maggie."

"Look, I'm sorry to involve ye. It was a mistake. I got desperate and was just hoping he'd go away since I still need to work with him, and he's clearly not picking up on my subtle clues. Or he's ignoring them." What a pain in the arse. She shouldn't have involved Conall. "I'll make it right and come clean with Andrew."

He shook his head, his gaze wandering before settling back on her. "Don't worry about it, aye? I don't like men who think they can pester women into dating them, and worse still, they don't tend to give up so easily. Seen too much of that with my younger sister and have little tolerance for it. But payback's a bitch, aye? I'll be expecting ye to take Piper for regular runs." Another smile—and damn if it didn't send her heartbeat thrumming.

"Does this mean ye'll actually pretend to be involved with me to keep him at bay?" He couldn't possibly mean it.

Conall shrugged. "For now."

CHAPTER Four

C ONALL WAS SURE he'd soon regret his decision to get involved, but he didn't like it when guys got pushy or insistent with women. Even now, with Maggie on his arm as they mingled with the other guests, Andrew's gaze still searched her out. He just hoped he wouldn't regret his decision to participate in this absurd charade. With luck, it'd be enough to make Andrew rethink the attention he'd been giving Maggie—or so he hoped.

He could easily suffer worse fates than spending time with the lass. He liked her, even if he hated to admit it. Not that he'd be pursuing anything with her.

He'd seen far too many relationships ruin good people, and though he may have thought he'd be able to escape such a fate when he'd been younger, he'd been proved wrong. He didn't need to get his heart broken more than once to know it wasn't an experience he wanted to repeat.

And frankly, he liked his life the way it was. He was set in his ways and the last thing he wanted was someone getting in his way and annoying him—someone who'd wake him up at six a.m.

So he'd play along for now and happily work by her side, but that was it.

Dinner was uneventful, other than the looks he was getting from Angus, Rowan, and Iain. Though once they moved to the library, it became clear that Andrew had yet to give up. The moment Conall left her side to get her a drink, Andrew sidled up to her—and he was ambushed by Rowan and Angus.

"Not a word from either of ye, aye? I'm in no mood." Conall knew they'd be curious as to what was happening between him and Maggie, but the last thing he wanted was to discuss a relationship that didn't exist.

"Och, now, ye don't really think we'd see ye cavorting with the pretty lass and not question ye about it? Especially when we thought the two of ye were single." Angus's lips twitched with humor, his blue eyes narrowing as he smiled.

"Well, I'm not buying it." Rowan smirked, her red hair aflame as it caught the firelight.

"Suit yerself. Now if ye'll excuse me, this conversation is over." Conall ignored their amused looks, and headed to Maggie in a futile attempt to save her.

Andrew looked like he had turned up the charm, smiling and leaning towards her, but Maggie was just standing there, a stiff smile on her lips, clearly humoring the man and far from enamored. Could he really be so clueless? Even a blind man could see she wasn't interested and was starting to lose her patience. No doubt it would have happened long ago if it wasn't for the fact that she'd need to continue working with the man.

Conall slipped to Maggie's side, his mood serious as he took Andrew in, and she turned the man down again.

"I'm afraid most of nights are spent preparing what I'll need for the job on the following day. I don't have a whole lot of time to myself, and what little time I do have, I'll be spending with Conall. He's promised to show me the latest in computer security and programming." She reached out and took Conall's hand, giving it a squeeze and tossing him a sultry smile that had his pulse jumping despite knowing it was nothing but a ruse. Her gaze lingered on him before slowly turning towards Andrew, as if she didn't want to look away. "Isn't that sweet of him to share his trade secrets?"

"Yeah—if you're into that sort of thing." Andrew looked over at Conall, smug. "Not exactly how I'd show a woman a good time."

Conall cocked his head, taking Andrew in. "I have no doubt—which is why she's with me." It was turning into a pissing match. Bloody hell. "If ye'll excuse us."

With their hands still linked, he escorted her away to a more private part of the library where they would, hopefully, be left alone. Before he could say anything, Maggie turned to face him, closing the distance between them.

"I'm so sorry to drag ye into this. This is only getting worse. Look, I'll deal with him on my own." Her brow was furrowed and her eyes had clouded over, refusing to look at him. "I should have never gotten ye involved."

Frankly, it pissed him off that some arse had gotten her this upset, or that it was even necessary for her to go to such measures. She'd turned Andrew down repeatedly—it should be more than enough to get it through his thick skull that she wasn't interested. "Ye can try to deal with it on yer own, but I doubt it'll do ye much good. He sees ye as a challenge, and I doubt he'll let up. As for not involving me, it's a bit too late for that, aye? And if I'm going to be dragged into this, then I sure as hell aren't going to let him bother ye."

"Conall…are ye sure? It'll be complicated because of work—and ye barely know me." She gave his hand a squeeze, and looked up at him with those big blue eyes and full kissable lips. "Not to mention this will put me in yer debt for such a bleeding long time, I'll end up having to permanently move to Dunmuir just so I can walk ye dog."

"Then it's a deal. That crazy mutt drives me nuts—and she likes ye. A lot." He brought their linked hands to his lips, ready to play his part. And though he knew they were doing nothing more than pretending, he couldn't fully ignore the way his body reacted when she smiled at him.

Maggie leaned in just a little, her curves brushing against his body. "How about we get out of here…'cause ye know, this little deal of ours could be a whole lot of fun." The way her lips turned up into a sultry smile and her eyes sparkled with mischief, he had no doubt he would thoroughly enjoy himself.

And yet…he should be keeping this relatively professional. It was one thing to hold hands and flirt, and another thing entirely to fall casually into bed with her, and then try to maintain a working relationship when it all went to hell—as it always did.

"Maybe a bit too much fun, aye? But if ye'd like to go, I'm happy to help ye escape." Now *that* suited him just fine, since he usually avoided these sorts of gatherings at all cost.

"Too much fun? There's no such thing." She went up on her toes to whisper in his ear, so the nearness of her—the way her curves brushed up against him, the way her warm breath on his skin sent a tingle through him—made him want to take her up on whatever it was she was offering. He may not be interested in complicating things between them, but he was no monk.

Yet in the end, logic and reason won out, even if he was sure he'd soon regret his decision when he was home alone. "Let's just get going. I don't know that anyone's buying us as a couple, and I doubt Andrew's going to stay away long."

"Maybe this will help convince them." She knotted her fists around his shirt and pulled him to her, her lips on his in a kiss that left him wanting to haul her to his bed. All coherent thought vanished, so it felt like there was no one in the room but the two of them—and nothing else mattered.

By the time she pulled away, he could barely think straight. "Bloody hell."

Her lips quirked into a playful smile. "Did ye want to rethink that bit about not having fun?"

"Aye, I may very well."

After making their escape, he let her talk him into going to the pub for a drink, though he insisted that she first drop off her bike at the cottage. Already dark out, it'd be too easy for her to take a spill with the roads always damp, especially when she was unfamiliar with the twists and turns.

They were down by the port of Dunmuir in no time at all. Though there weren't many young people who lived in the area, there seemed to be more and more tourists coming to visit since Cat and Iain found the Highlander's Hope. The one pub in town was busy even for a Friday night, though they managed to find a spot at the bar.

"What will ye have?" Of course, Lara was working, which meant the rumor mill would be churning about him being in Maggie's company. Well, let them talk. Not like he gave a rat's arse what they said.

Maggie climbed onto the stool with a smile. "A pint of the black stuff, if ye'd be so kind."

"And a whisky, Lara. Thanks." Conall turned towards Maggie and finally took a good look at her, now that he had the chance to do so without Andrew interrupting them.

Up until now, she'd been dressed casually every time he'd seen her, either for work or her run. Tonight, however, she'd set free that gorgeous thick mane, and her blue eyes and full lips were accented just enough to make them sparkle.

Though she was pretty, it was more than that. There was something about her that made people stop and take notice. Perhaps it wasn't her beauty but rather the fierce intelligence in her eyes. Or maybe the way she always seemed animated—alive with humor and passion, with desire.

And damn…that kiss of hers had left one hell of an impression. Enough so that all kisses from his past and all kisses in his future would now be compared to hers—and would likely fall short. Yet with fire like that, it was far too easy to get burned, to be scarred with wounds that might never heal.

Hadn't he seen it with his very own father? In love with someone who couldn't love him back. Sure, he'd gone on to marry his mother afterwards, but it was clear she would never be enough to erase his loss. Of course, his father tried to make it work and he loved his children, but his marriage was doomed to fail. Conall's mother eventually divorced him, yet another heart broken.

"Are ye all right? Ye've gone all quiet on me—and seeing that ye don't say a whole lot to begin with, ye've got me worried." Her brows had drawn together over her darkened eyes and her full lips were twisted in a pout. "I dated a mime who said more than you do."

"Funny." He managed a bit of a smile, trying to set her mind at ease. "So, do ye do many of these jobs on yer own? I can't imagine it's the first time ye've had to deal with men like Andrew."

She shrugged with a tilt of her head, so her amber-colored locks fell over her shoulder. "My brother eventually shows up, but ye'd be right. There are far too many arses and clueless men. I do my best to ignore them if at all possible, and I can usually handle myself if things escalate. It's usually best to avoid letting things get to that stage, though—which is why I truly appreciate yer help."

"I've got a younger sister, aye? I'd hate to think of her in a similar situation and no one willing to help."

Lara slid their drinks in front of them with a teasing smile, clearly up to no good. "Are ye not going to introduce us to yer lass, Conall? And that being a rare sight. Can't remember the last time ye brought someone around."

"Do ye wonder why, Lara? Really?" He knew better than to let her get to him, but after a lifetime of dealing with her, his patience had worn thin. Being of the same age, they'd been in school together since the age of five.

"I'm Maggie—and I take it yer Lara. It's a pleasure." Maggie reached out and shook Lara's hand with a smile before turning back to Conall. "And don't you know better than to get on the wrong side of the woman who serves the pints in town?"

"I like her, Conall. A lot. She might be just the thing ye need." And just like a tornado setting down to inflict its damage for a few moments, Lara was off to wreak her havoc elsewhere.

Conall shook his head and took a long draw from his glass, the heat of the whisky melting its way down his throat to his core. And then he noticed Maggie was looking at him with a grin twitching at her lips, refusing to be contained. "What?"

"Ye're too serious, love. Might have to make it my mission to see ye lighten up and start living yer life to its fullest. Could be the perfect way to pay ye back." Her eyebrows flicked up with mischief and humor.

"I like my life just the way it is, thank ye very much." He had to laugh, finding it difficult to stay annoyed when she was in such a good mood. "Ye do understand that if I wanted my life to be any different, then I'd have changed it, aye?"

"See…already that's so much better. Ye've got a great smile, love. Can't go blaming a girl for wanting to see it." She took a long draw from her pint and then turned those ice blue eyes on him, her gaze locked on his. "And I like ye, Conall. A lot. Question is, what are ye going to do about it?"

Bloody hell. He shook his head, another smile on his lips despite himself. "Are ye always this forward?"

"I can be when I find someone I connect with. It doesn't happen often, mind ye, but if it does, I'm not one to let things pass me by. We only get to live this life once, so we might as well make the best of it." She gave him another one of her perky smiles before taking another sip of her pint. "I can be patient if ye need more time, though."

He'd love to take her up on her offer, but…he couldn't. Women like Maggie were dangerous. Addictive. And he'd gotten burned bad enough to know he should stay away. Not to mention they were working together, and would be for several more months. Things could get uncomfortable if it all went bad. "I'd be a fool to turn ye down, lass. Yet I could do with a wee bit more time, if ye're offering."

She looked up at him through thick lashes, the corners of her kissable lips turning up in a smile. "I can live with that, though I'll tell ye now, I'm not known for my patience."

"I ne'er would've guessed it."

CHAPTER
Five

MAGGIE HAD BEEN running cables and wiring all day long—which also meant she'd been dealing with Andrew. Under normal circumstances, she knew Andrew would likely leave most of the work he'd been doing to his crew, but that wouldn't afford him enough opportunity to try to wear her down. She'd spent the day trying to be civil with the man, but her patience was wearing thin.

"Come on, Maggie. It's getting late and you've got to eat. Let me buy you dinner." Andrew leaned against the worktable, his arms crossed in front of his chest and his long legs stretched out in front of him, a flirty smile on his lips.

"I've got work I need to wrap up after I finish with the wiring, and already have dinner plans." She barely looked up at him, and instead concentrated on her connections, her movements tense as annoyance set in. "If ye don't mind, I need to focus on this so I can get out of here."

"Dinner with…what's his name? Conall, right?" Andrew looked smug when she threw a glare in his direction. "You don't really think I believe the two of you are together, do you?"

She stood, her jaw clenched and her muscles coiled, her eyes locked on his, tired of being polite. "Frankly, I don't give a shite what ye believe. I'm not interested in dinner or a pint with ye. Not now. Not ever. Now if ye don't mind, I'd like to finish up without having to make up yet another excuse to avoid yer company."

His hand shot out and grabbed her by the arm, stepping towards her, his words forced past a clenched jaw. "Who the hell do you think you are, speaking to me like that?"

"I'm the person who's going to make ye sorry if ye don't let go of my arm." He was really pissing her off. No more being nice—even if she had to work with him. He'd just crossed the line.

He let go of her arm, looking stunned, as if realizing what he'd just done. "I'm so sorry…I don't know what came over me."

"Maggie…are ye in here?" Conall was calling her from the hall, and it was clear he'd be there in a matter of seconds.

Andrew took a step back, still looking shaken, and without another word, headed off in the opposite direction just as Conall walked into the room.

Conall watched as Andrew left out one of the side doors before turning to look at her, his gaze wandering over her face, her body. "Hey, are ye all right? Ye look a bit shaken."

"I'm not shaken, I'm furious." Despite Andrew's apology, she was pissed off—but the last thing she wanted was to involve Conall further than she already had. Shite. She shouldn't have said anything—not that he couldn't see something was wrong, and the obvious reason for it would be Andrew. "It's nothing."

"Maggie, ye know I'm neither blind nor a fool, right?" He shook his head, his lips pursed into a tight line.

"Don't suppose ye'd like to get out of here and grab a bite to eat? I have a few steaks at the cottage." She really could do with the distraction of his company. If not, she'd just stew over the incident with Andrew and play out the details in her head, wondering if there had been any way to avoid things getting to this point.

His eyebrows rose in a way that reminded her of the nuns who used to teach at her elementary school. "I'm not letting ye off the hook, but I will take ye up on dinner since I'd rather not cook if I don't have to. Just have to head home and let Piper out first."

"Why don't ye bring her with ye? We could take her out for a walk afterwards."

"Aye, maybe I will."

Though they parted ways, he stood there waiting to make sure she got on her bike and was still watching her as she took off down the road. She thought the gesture sweet. Still…the incident with Andrew left her not wanting to involve Conall any more than she already had, and that probably meant that falling into his bed for a romp might not be wise. Things had a tendency to get complicated once you threw sex into the mix, and Conall already seemed complicated enough on his own, without helping the matter along.

Once home, she got started on dinner, knowing she'd be able to forget her troubles if she focused on cooking. She liked that despite living in the cottage for only a few weeks, it was already feeling more like home, rather than another place to just rest her head. It was also nice that the additional bedroom would give Liam a place to stay once he wrapped up the updates for their other client. Constantly working together, she missed her brother when he wasn't around, even if he could be a pain in the arse.

Maggie jacked up the temperature on the Aga and quickly tossed together the ingredients for a traditional Irish brown bread, knowing it would bake up in time to be served with the rest of their meal. Inspired, she figured an Irish theme would be appropriate and got started on the colcannon next. With the potatoes boiling, she caramelized some onions, sautéed some kale, and browned some crispy bacon, setting them aside to add to the potatoes once they'd been mashed with butter and cream. It'd be a perfect accompaniment to the steak, well-seasoned and cooked to medium-rare.

Dinner was nearly ready by the time Conall showed up with a bottle of wine and Piper in tow. "Hope a Merlot will work for ye."

"Sounds perfect." Maggie gave Piper a good scratch, and then unhooked her leash. But when she stood, it was to find him looking at her with his brow furrowed. "What's wrong?"

"I don't appreciate ye not being honest with me about what happened today with Andrew." His gold eyes pinned her to the spot, though she was in no mood to rehash things. One hell of a way to start the evening, too.

"Listen, love. It's been a rough day and I'd rather not dwell on it." She spun to head into the kitchen when he grabbed her hand.

"That's not how I work, Maggie. I don't like secrets or half-truths. Not with lovers, nor my friends. And since ye've involved me in this thing with Andrew, then I'd appreciate some honesty."

"And *I* don't like rehashing things that are of no consequence. I never should have involved ye in this mess and for that I truly am sorry. I'm not normally one for regrets, Conall, but bleedin' hell…if I could change it, I would." She let out a frustrated sigh. What the hell was she supposed to do? Not like she could turn back time—and there was no point in upsetting him. Telling him what happened would only involve him further and escalate things with Andrew. "I'm going to burn the food."

She made her escape into the kitchen and busied herself with the finishing touches on dinner, though she could feel his hard gaze on her.

"I'm not letting this go, Maggie. You got me involved and now that I am, I want the truth, damn it. I'll not wander about clueless to what's happening around me—especially when I'm mixed up in this mess." He closed the distance between them, his movements stiff, contained, his voice strained under the control he was exerting. "Ye owe me that at least."

What the hell were they arguing about? It was clear he had a tendency to get annoyed pretty quickly, but she hadn't expected to see any real heat—or passion—from him. The man was getting more interesting by the moment. Not that she would take advantage of all that pent-up tension. Nope—not at all.

With her arms crossed in front of her chest, she cocked her head and pinned him with a stare, her lips curling in amusement. "Ye're awfully persuasive, love, and sexy to boot. But if ye think I'm going to involve ye any further than I already have, then you can guess again. I may have screwed up by dragging ye into this, but I try to learn from my mistakes and I won't let ye get caught up in this mess more than ye already are. Now if ye don't mind, I've got dinner to serve."

Ignoring the curses he was mumbling under his breath, she turned back to the stove and pulled out the plates she had heating, setting them aside. Before she could reach for anything else, he spun her around and pulled her close.

Her breath caught as he covered her mouth with his—taking, tasting—his stubble rough against her soft skin, a hint of pain to heighten the pleasure and send a shudder of need through her body. Fisting her hair, he pulled her head back to feast on her neck, nipping down the length of it, causing goose bumps to dance across her skin.

His kiss deepened as he pushed her against the counter so her world fell away, so there was nothing but him, his hard muscular form, tense, pressed against hers, fueling her desires. She ran her hands down his chest and to his hips, pulling him closer. By the gods, she wanted him something fierce, then and there, dinner be damned.

He pulled away just enough to break off their kiss, looked at her as if he'd devour her in a heartbeat, took yet another hard kiss, and then stepped away, leaving her reeling and desperate for him.

His breathing was still heavy when he pinned her with a hard stare. "Don't ye dare tell me Andrew doesn't concern me—because it does, damn it. Now ye better tell me what the hell happened or ye're on yer own."

After that kiss, his ultimatum was like a slap to the face, her shock warring with her anger. Well, she had more than enough of a temper to match his. "Like that, is it? Ye think you can just kiss me and then make demands? Well, I already told you I don't need yer help, so you can go to hell, Conall Stewart. Get out. And don't go thinking I'll be coming by to walk yer dog, either."

"Good! Maybe I'll finally get a bit of peace and quiet instead of getting woken up at the crack of dawn."

And just like that, he grabbed Piper and left, not another word spoken between them.

Maggie's argument with Conall had put her in a sour mood, and with his end of the job easily managed from home, Conall had done just that. She hadn't seen or heard from him in days, which of course only made things worse. If he did ever show up again, she knew she'd somehow manage to smooth things between them, even if she was still annoyed with him—and herself, truth be told—for the stupid argument and a ruined dinner.

She debated showing up at his house to call a truce, but her pride got in the way. As far as she was concerned, she was right to not involve him further. With three brothers, she knew well enough that things would escalate if she told Conall that Andrew had grabbed her arm, even if the man had already apologized—not that it justified what he'd done.

Even the job seemed to be protesting her crankiness. She kept hitting one snag after another, which did little to improve her disposition. What she needed to do was concentrate on the reason she was in Dunmuir—and that had nothing to do with Conall. He was nothing but a distraction who'd ruined her happy-go-lucky mood. And with the problems that kept popping up all over the jobsite, she had to stay focused.

Doing her best to ignore her thoughts of Conall, she got back to work on the display case where they'd be housing the Highlander's Hope, fingers crossed that nothing would go wrong. She pulled on her welding mask and with sparks flying, finished the metal housing that would hold all the detectors used in keeping the jewels safe. Turning off the torch, she popped her visor back, happy for the fresh air. Yanking off her gloves, she turned towards her tools and ran right into Andrew.

"Easy there." He held onto her as if she might lose her balance and tumble, though his touch had her stiffening, her anger sparking.

She took a step back and out of his arms, her brow furrowed with annoyance. "What can I do for ye?"

"Been in Glasgow the last few days, and didn't like the way things played out between us the last time I'd seen you. I wanted to apologize for being an ass. What you do outside of work is none of my business, and I get that you're not interested." She didn't say anything, still not trusting him. He shrugged and took a step back. "I guess that's it. Again, sorry for causing you trouble."

He turned to go, but she now felt guilty for not saying anything. "Thanks—for the apology."

He looked over his shoulder and nodded before continuing on his way.

CHAPTER Six

ONALL WAS IN no mood to deal with Rowan, who'd dropped by unannounced. "I'm working."

Not that she cared. She wandered in past him, red hair bouncing, and plopped herself on the sofa. Seizing the opportunity, Piper jumped up where she didn't belong, and nestled against Rowan, who gave her a rough scratch behind the pup's floppy tan ears. "Hadn't seen or heard from you since the party, so I figured I'd check in. See what you're up to."

"What I'm up to is trying to get some work done—and I can't do that if ye're here to harass me." He pulled Piper off the sofa and sat down next to Rowan. "Shouldn't ye be bugging Angus?"

"He's out on a complicated foaling a few hours north of here. Probably won't be back until late tonight." Shifting to sit sideways, she slung her elbow over the back of the sofa and propped her head in her hand, her eyes sparkling with mischief. "So…where's Maggie?"

He glared at her, though it resulted in nothing more than Rowan's smile widening. "How would I know? Did ye try the cottage?"

"Crap. Has it already gone to hell? What did you do?" When his glare turned to a scowl, she gave him half a pout, her brows drawn over those bright green eyes. "Oh, come on, Conall. You know you can talk to me. After Angus, you're my best friend."

"Then that's a sad state of affairs, ain't it?" He let out a weary sigh, guilt nagging him for pushing Rowan away. "What do ye want me to say? You were right that night at the party—there was nothing going on between us. Some bloke was bothering her, and I was a convenient ploy to be rid of him."

Rowan shook her head no, sending her loose curls spilling over her shoulder. "She may have been trying to avoid this other guy, but I saw the kiss she planted on you, and I can tell you now, the girl likes you."

"She may have at one point in time, but I've since managed to muck things up. Not like it matters, aye? She'll be gone in a few months' time, and it's not like I need the headache of a relationship." Yet the mere mention of Maggie had him thinking of how she felt in his arms when he kissed her. The way her curves fit against his body. How his heart tripped over itself as their kiss deepened and she pulled him close.

Rowan let out a sigh and leaned forward. "You can't have screwed up that badly, Conall. And don't go giving me that crap about not wanting a relationship. No one wants to be alone, and frankly, it would do you a world of good to have a bit of fun. Not to mention, get laid."

His head was now throbbing. "Rowan, I swear ye'd drive a man to drink."

"Aw. You're so sweet." She leaned forward and kissed his cheek before getting to her feet. "Call her, Conall—or even better, pay her a visit. 'Cause if you don't, then I'm afraid I'll be forced to meddle. And you wouldn't want that, now would you?"

He had to laugh. "You're such a pain in the arse, lass."

"And yet you still love me."

Conall wandered through the jobsite, and though he told himself he was there purely for work, he found his gaze wandering about with the hope of seeing Maggie. Not that he'd be apologizing, since he'd done nothing wrong. But he did need to keep things civil between the two of them. They still had to work together, and the longer they went without seeing each other, the more awkward it would be.

Though he didn't immediately see her when he entered the main room, he felt her presence. And then he spotted her, a small smile upon her lips as she stood there—speaking to Andrew, of all people. His chest tightened and his muscles stiffened as he fought to extinguish the spark of jealousy that threatened to ignite.

He thought about continuing on his way, but she looked over at him, and then smiled—the kind that reached her eyes and made them sparkle like the summer sun on a lake. He let out a deep breath as she excused herself to Andrew, and started heading in his direction.

"Hey there. Been a while." She reached out and gave his hand a quick squeeze before letting it go. "Hope ye've been keeping well."

His gaze flicked to Andrew, who was watching them. "See ye've patched things up with yer friend there."

He didn't like the man. And it went well past any jealousy he might harbor when it came to seeing him with Maggie. Maybe it had to do with one too many jerks, just like Andrew, giving his sister a hard time. But this wasn't his sister and he should let it go. Let Maggie do whatever she damn well pleased. Instead, he found himself wanting to punch Andrew before tossing Maggie over his shoulder and dragging her to his bed to claim her as his own.

"He apologized for being pushy, and I figured since I still have to work with him for several more months, it might be best to let it go and try to get along. Surely you can see the merit in that. No?"

"Och, aye. I'm sure he truly means it, too." Bloody hell. How was it the woman always got his back up? And in such short time. He'd barely known the lass a few weeks, yet she'd already gotten under his skin. "Sorry. Not like it's any of my business. You can do as ye damn well please. But if ye have a moment and can pull yerself away from yer newfound friend, I need to go over a few changes I'd like to make to the security schematics."

"Pull myself away, is it? And do as I damn well please?" Her eyebrows flicked up as she pinned him with a glare, her jaw tight. "Ye know ye can be a real arse, Conall."

He shrugged, annoyed with himself for upsetting her when there was no need for it. "So can we get to work or do ye have other plans?"

She made a production of checking her watch. "It's a bit late, don't ye think?"

Bollocks. He hadn't really checked the time, and it was already after five. "Tomorrow then."

Silently cursing, he turned to go when a capable hand grabbed his arm and he found himself looking into her blue eyes, those full kissable lips of hers curling in a shadow of a smile. It was all he could do to not pull her to him and cover her mouth with his, desperate to have her in his arms. He wanted to kiss her until she yielded, wanted to take her pressed against the wall or bent over the table. She called out to every primal urge in him and it took all he had to resist her.

With her head cocked and one brow perked, she stood there, arms crossed, leaving him to wonder if she could read his mind—to wonder if she was aware of the effect she had on him. "You owe me for a ruined meal—one I worked hard on, mind ye—and since ye don't like to cook, ye'll be buying me dinner."

"Am I now?" A smile pulled at the corners of his mouth as he was left shaking his head and wondering how the hell she'd snuck in past his defenses and left him falling for her. He might be damn good at securing any type of network or server, but he'd left himself wide open.

She linked her arm with his, moving them towards the door. "I wasn't asking, love."

He was happy to play her games—for now. "Does this mean I'm forgiven?"

"Forgiven?" The sideways glance she gave him and her mischievous laugh had a ball of heat and need knotting in his stomach. "And miss out on all the fun of doling out yer punishment while you're tied to my bed? I don't think so."

Bloody hell. He didn't think they'd even make it home if she kept this up. "If there's someone here who'll be tied to a bed, it's not me, lass."

"Promises, promises." When she leaned into him, the warmth of her body, the feel of her on his arm, sent his pulse hammering and his cock growing hard. "So where are ye taking me?"

He did his best to clear his head, to focus on what she was saying instead of what she'd look like splayed naked on his bed. "Ye do realize there aren't a whole lot of restaurants in town. Ye've got yer choice of the pub or the chipper." Conall tried to think of other alternatives, but food was *not* what he wanted after their taunts.

Stepping out into the brisk September air coming in off the sea, he steered them towards his car, conveniently parked near her deathtrap of a bike.

She grabbed her helmet, and turned to face him so the sun escaping through the clouds picked up the flecks of gold in her eyes and illuminated the blue. "Well, if ye wanted to get some work done over dinner, then we could grab something at the chipper and take it back to your place or mine."

"The chipper it is then." He breathed in the cool damp air in a futile attempt to clear his head and rein in his thoughts. If he kept up on the road he was on—if he gave in to the overwhelming need he had of her—he knew he'd eventually regret it. Women like Maggie broke hearts. Shattered them to smithereens. And his heart was already weary and battle-scarred.

Yet by the time they abandoned her bike, grabbed the food and headed back to his house, he'd had enough time to start second-guessing himself. With her at his side, all thoughts of keeping his distance washed away on a wave of need.

He knew it'd be a mistake, and yet he liked her—a lot. Far more than he should or was wise. Then again, it'd be easy enough to just enjoy the time they had together. It's not like she'd be around past the New Year. Still…something nagged at the back of his mind and in the pit of his gut, telling him it could all go cursedly wrong. A woman like Maggie? You couldn't play with fire and not get burned.

Maggie sat by his side, munching on her fish and chips and tossing Piper the occasional treat, while he pulled out the plans and looked them over. Not that he could concentrate on the task at hand when he was distracted by thoughts of impending doom and a primal need to get her naked. Bollocks.

"Leave it for now—your fish is getting cold. Nothing tastes worse once it gets soggy." Maggie shifted towards him, sitting sideways, with her plate in her lap. "There's plenty of time for work—and fun—later. Besides, ye'll want to keep yer energy up."

"Will I, now? And do I get a say regarding the night's entertainment?" He shouldn't be playing this game, and yet…Damn. She was smart, pretty and fun, and in many ways far safer than getting involved with anyone else, since she'd soon be gone.

Her eyes widened and sparkled with mischief as she munched on a chip, a teasing smile on her lips. "Not if yer tied to the bed, ye don't."

His skin felt too tight to contain the need and energy that coursed through him. He had to admire such boldness, and it only added to the growing attraction he was desperately trying to ignore. "Are ye always such a flirt?"

She shrugged. "Like I've said before—there's no point in not making the most of the opportunities that come our way. That said, I'm damn picky, if it makes ye feel any better. And you, me dear, make the cut—and then some."

She set aside her plate and then put his on the end table, out of the dog's reach, before slipping one long leg over his lap to straddle him, the weight and heat of her supple body having an immediate effect. A surge of need coursed through him as he ached to have her, his pulse pounding and his heart thrashing against his ribs as he fought to take a breath. There was no chance of coherent thought. No chance he could resist her even if he wanted to—not that he did. It felt too right. Too perfect.

He sat forward so she was but a breath away, her breasts pressed against him as he slipped his hands down the length of her back, settling on her waist to pull her even closer. With a teasing smile, she shifted her hips against his hard length, so he could think of nothing but ravaging her. It had been months since he'd last been with anyone, and now no one but Maggie would do. He was going to have her in a most thorough manner and wouldn't let up until he'd explored every inch of her, until she was laying there spent and utterly satisfied, until she could utter no one's name but his.

Her hair fell forward as she leaned over and kissed him, the scent of coconut and lime filling his head, their kiss deepening. By the gods, he wanted her, and with the heat of her pressed against him and her lips tasting like honey fresh from the comb, there was no possible way he could take this slow. Not that it mattered. Maggie didn't seem to have much patience either, her hands already running down his chest and pulling his shirt up over his head.

He followed suit, quickly ridding her of her top, his thumbs brushing against her hard nipples through her red lacy bra, eliciting a moan from her sweet lips. A flick of the clasp, and he set her glorious breasts free— when a buzzing vibration sounded.

She pulled away and dug out her phone as he continued to trail kisses down her neck. "Fuck."

"Ignore it." He held her close, his words coming out in a murmur against her soft skin.

With a hand on his chest, she pushed him away. "I can't. Sorry. It's my bus with all the tech in it. There's been some sort of disturbance."

She was already sliding off his lap with a string of curses that alternated between English and Irish as she pulled on her bra, and he caught one last glimpse of her perfectly pert breasts. He groaned, desperately trying to ignore the pulsing ache between his legs that threatened to overtake him. "I'm coming with ye."

"Ye don't have to. I can come back once I get it sorted." She turned her shirt the right way out, and pulled it on while he grabbed his own and got dressed.

His temper sparked to think she'd just leave him behind when the security of *their* project might be in jeopardy—*and* that she'd run into a potentially dangerous situation on her own without giving it a second thought. As if he'd just sit there on the sofa with a hard on, casually waiting for her return while she dealt with who the hell knows what.

"I'm coming with ye, Maggie. Does your phone tell ye what sort of disturbance it is?" Conall was sure she had all sorts of information being sent through to her smartphone.

"From the readings it's giving me, there hasn't been a breach, but there was an attempt at the door. It sounds an alarm if it's been tampered with, so it may have scared off whoever was snooping." She threw on her jacket, and was already heading for the door, leaving him to catch up. "I've got surveillance cameras there, but I'm not seeing anything over the feed that's being sent to my phone. Once I've got the actual footage, we should be able to zoom in and see what happened."

That was something, at least. They could figure out exactly what happened rather than guessing.

He found himself admiring how thorough she was with her work, and damn if it didn't make him like her all the more—beyond the lust and want. That fact that she could be both serious about some things and yet still have a playful side made her all the more intriguing.

With her bike still at the cottage, he drove, though it left her antsy and on edge, her entire body taut. She glared at him. "Could ye not drive just a wee bit faster?"

"Ye need to calm yerself, love. We're nearly there, aye?" Under normal circumstances he'd be annoyed, but humor tugged at his lips. "Are ye always this impatient?"

"What if I am? No point in wasting time when it could be better spent doing other things. This wasn't in my plans for the evening." She looked over at him through her thick lashes, the corners of her mouth teasing into a smile. "So don't hold it against me if I'd like to wrap things up and get back to what we were doing."

"Ye'll hear no complaints from me, lass." He looked over at her with a grin tugging at his lips while his gaze drank her in, and left him wondering if he'd ever get his fill. Bloody hell, she was something. An athletic build with just enough curves, thick gorgeous hair, lips that made you want to bite them and those eyes—eyes that reached his very soul and left him unable to look away.

"Ye've got a great smile, Conall. It's a pity it doesn't come out to play more often."

Another smile sprung to his lips. "Maybe you can change that for me."

CHAPTER
Seven

AGGIE WALKED TOWARDS Andrew, who was standing by her bus, the tension between him and Conall palpable. "What happened? Did ye see?"

"Unfortunately not. The alarm sounded as I was wrapping up my own work, so I came out to investigate. Didn't see anything out of the ordinary, though." He stuffed his hands in his jean pockets and shrugged. "Wish I could be of more help. Anything I can do?"

"I can manage, but appreciate the offer." She gave him a small smile and then moved to the door of her bus to take a closer look.

At first glance all seemed normal, except for the red light blinking above the lock, keypad, and biometric scanner. Needing to make sure there wasn't any other area breached, she slowly wandered around the vehicle, checking the windows and the lower compartments before circling to the front. "Someone tried to get in here at the door—the light would be green otherwise—but I don't think they disturbed any other area. I'll need to check the surveillance feed, though."

She pulled out her keys, found the one she needed, inserted and turned it, before putting her hand on the scanner. A beam of white light ran the length of her hand and then turned green. Lastly, she put in the override code that was needed due to the tripped alarm, though she took care to block the numbers from view. It wasn't that she didn't trust Conall, but one could never be too safe, and more so, Andrew had yet to leave.

With the alarm off, she opened the door and climbed onto the first step. Conall followed behind her, but she didn't want Andrew joining them. "Thanks, Andrew. We can take care of it from here."

He nodded. "Let me know if there's an issue. If someone's snooping around, I need to know."

"Will do." Maggie waited for him to go, let Conall pass, and then locked the door behind them.

Space was tight with her equipment and tools stacked floor to ceiling within their customized compartments. A desk with her computer systems was nestled in one of the corners; four touch screen monitors splayed out in front of her. She wheeled a chair over to Conall, and grabbed the one already tucked in at the desk. With a few taps of the keys, she had the video surveillance files pulled up.

She plugged in the approximate time of the disturbance and focused on the view surrounding her bus, taken from multiple angles with enough overlap to avoid blind spots. There was no one around, so she slowly sped through the recording. Once they got close to the time they were looking for, she slowed the speed. Not long after, the screens turned to snow, the image on each of the multiple cameras gone.

She cursed. Repeatedly. And every way she knew how. "This was no accident. Someone sent an electrical pulse through to the cameras. I don't know how they managed it, but they did."

He ran a hand across his heavily stubbled jaw. "Or it could be a surge, and that's what triggered the alarm. No?"

"Maybe, though there are safeguards in place to keep that from happening—surge protectors, back-up batteries and generators." Yet she knew nothing was foolproof, and power could easily surge this far out in the woods, especially when the wiring that'd been run in from the road was still new. "I guess there could be glitches in the new wiring that still need to be worked out, but I don't like it."

They continued to watch as the images came back, an alarm now sounding. Before long, Andrew showed up on the screen and checked on the disturbance. There was nothing else. "We should probably call Iain."

"Aye. He should know. It could be nothing, but I like to keep him informed." Conall pulled out his phone and left Iain a message. "What would ye like to do?"

That was a good question. The alarm going off left her uneasy enough to not want to leave things unguarded. "Would ye hate me if I told ye I'd need to cancel our date for the evening? I think I'm going to spend the night here. I don't want to leave this place unattended."

"Or we could just drive it to my house. It's got wheels, aye?" The corners of his mouth turned up in another one of those once-thought-elusive smiles.

"Ye know, I like ye more and more with each passing moment." Though she'd only been looking for a way to keep herself from getting bored while working the job, Conall had turned out to be a pleasant surprise.

"If ye like me now, just wait until I'm through with ye later tonight." His eyes sparkled, alight as if they were a glass of whisky caught in the glow of a fire.

She ran a hand over his thick stubble, loving his scruffy good looks and his intensity—from his sharp gaze to his stern demeanor even. She leaned in and kissed him. "Ye know…ye look more like a fisherman—or even a highwayman of old—rather than a computer genius."

"Do I, now?" He tucked a loose strand of hair behind her ear as his touch lingered and his eyes met hers, making her want to kiss him again.

"Yeah…Far too rugged and fit for that sort of thing. So, how the hell is it that ye're single?" Good looking, smart, well off, and successful—granted he lived out in the middle of nowhere, but still.

"I like it that way, lass." He let out a weary sigh, his smile fading like a dream vanishing upon awaking.

There was more he wasn't telling her. The slump in his shoulders, the way his eyes clouded over…he might be single, but there was a reason for it. He'd been burned—bad enough to have him rethinking relationships altogether. She could certainly relate. There was a reason she refused to let life pass her by, and that was because she'd done just that for far too long.

She'd given her all to Oliver, only to find she was the only one trying, the only one giving her love fully. It'd left her hurt, heartbroken, depressed and cynical—until she woke up one morning and decided she'd wasted enough of her life in a bad relationship and pining over a man who wasn't worthy of her. From that day forward, she decided she wouldn't squander a single moment. She was happy to have fun until she found someone worthy of her love, but once she found that person, she needed to know they wouldn't be loving her in half-measures. She deserved better than that.

Good thing Conall was just a bit of fun. Not that he couldn't easily be more if circumstances were different. But she'd be gone before long—and that was probably for the best since he clearly didn't want anything more serious. In a few months, she'd be off to the job she had booked in London.

She managed a smile, pushing her thoughts to the side. "Are ye still ready to pick up where we left off?"

"Aye, lass. I am if you are."

She was—wasn't she? A nagging feeling told her she might be playing a dangerous game. Conall was rugged, brilliant, and gilded as if touched by the gods. With his amber eyes and honey hair, she could easily fall for him—hard.

"Yeah, I think I am. I won't be too far behind ye with the bus. Just need to switch over to the generator and disconnect my power supply." She stood and pushed aside her doubts. She needed fun and distraction in the form of sex. It was nothing more than that.

"I can wait for ye." He got to his feet but his brow furrowed as he pursed his lips. Brushing her cheek, his hand warm and just a little rough, his eyes locked on hers. "Listen, love, if ye're not up for tonight, we can leave it for another time, aye? There's no point in doing this if ye're distracted with work. It can wait. I'm patient enough."

She reached up and linked her hand around his arm as he cupped the back of her neck. Her cursed thoughts were still nagging at her. Between worrying about the alarm and whether or not she was falling for Conall too hard and too fast, going home with him might not be the smartest move.

"I'm sorry. My head's just in a weird place. Doubt I'd be much fun." When he brushed a thumb across her cheek, she leaned against his hand, her eyes closing for a moment.

He frowned, his eyes searching her face. "Let me stay with ye. Here. Just as a friend—a coworker. Can't say why, but ye have me worried, love."

She wanted to tell him to stay, especially when her mind had already drifted to thoughts of what it would be like to have him wrapped around her body, holding her tightly. But she knew it would do nothing but leave her wanting him even more—and not just for a bit of a fling. It may have started that way—hell, just a few hours ago, she'd have said that was all she wanted—but she had realized somewhere along the way that she was starting to fall for him, and it would be one hell of a slippery slope, her demise quick, especially when he'd made it clear he was interested in nothing serious.

"I really appreciate it, Conall. I do. But…" Was she being stupid? Paranoid? It'd be so damn easy to just lean forward and kiss him. Long. Hard. And even easier to drag him to the back of the bus and the bed. Damn. She bit her lip to keep from kissing him.

"But…ye'll see me in the morning." He leaned in and kissed the tip of her nose. "No worries, aye? Just keep my number handy. If the alarm trips again, I don't want ye heading to check it out on yer own. Ye call me, and I'll be over in a matter of minutes."

"I promise."

After seeing Conall off, Maggie decided to recheck her systems to try to figure out what set off the alarms and why her cameras shorted. It didn't make sense that a power surge would knock them out when she had two back-up power supplies. Something else must have happened, but what? She started up some scans of the system, and while those were running, got herself a Guinness with a shot of black currant syrup.

There was a knock at the door, and she half hoped Conall had come back to keep her company, despite the fact that she'd been the one to send him away. Of course she couldn't possibly be that lucky. She let out a sigh when she pulled up the view of the security camera and found Andrew at her door. It'd be easy enough to ignore him since the windows were tinted and he couldn't see in, except for the small fact that he'd seen her go in and would know she was ignoring him.

Damn. She opened the door and managed a smile. "Hey."

"Saw Conall leave and wanted to make sure you were all set with the alarm. Anything I can do to help?" He shifted his weight and looked up at her while she stood on the steps of the bus, his brown eyes nearly black in the dim of dusk.

Maggie shrugged. "I'm not quite sure what happened. Probably a power surge that managed to short out the entire system. It's unusual but not completely out of the question, I suppose."

"You've got my number if you need it, right?" Indeed, she had numbers to almost everyone working the job. He gave her a crooked smile. "And don't worry—I won't ask you out again for a drink. I get that you're not interested."

"Andrew…" She felt guilty.

He looked down at his feet before glancing up at her out of the corner of his eye. "You're with Conall, right? I get it. Not like I haven't had girls turn me down before—though they're not usually as pretty as you."

More guilt. "Look…I don't know what to tell ye. I don't want things to be awkward when we're stuck working together for the next few months. And yes—I'm with Conall."

"I know—and I promise not to be a pain again. It's just that I've sort of been on my own up here. My boss doesn't say much, and the crew we've hired is fairly local, so they head home. Really…I didn't mean to go bugging you, and I can't apologize enough for grabbing your arm. I'm mortified." With his eyes on the ground, he shook his head, his shoulders slumped. "I've just been lonely."

All she wanted was for him to go, yet she now found herself feeling sorry for the guy. She let out a weary sigh, hoping she wouldn't regret being friendly. "I just poured myself a pint. Could scavenge another glass if ye're interested—though it's nothing more than just a drink between colleagues."

His smile widened, his eyebrows flicking up for a second. "Never been one to turn down a drink—especially when it's between colleagues."

Stepping to the side to let him pass, his body brushed against hers in the confines of the tight space. She locked the door and secured the systems before following Andrew into the main galley. "I've got Guinness, Boddington's, hard cider, and Jameson."

"Boddington's, if you don't mind." He looked around and let out a whistle. "Bloody hell, this is a lot of equipment."

"Yeah. Goes with the job." She reached over and flicked off the monitors before grabbing him his beer. "Here ye go."

"It's a pretty nice setup, though. Better than some of the places I've been forced to sleep in when on a job." He leaned against the bank of seats, his long legs crossed out in front of him. "Iain's been nice enough to set us up in one of the cottages not far from here. Share the space with a few of the other guys on the nights they stick around—which has its moments."

She had to laugh. She knew exactly what it was like to live in a house full of men. "Which is probably why you keep trying to escape to the pub."

"Well, you're certainly better company and a hell of a lot better-looking than that lot, so I hope you don't blame me for my enthusiasm." He cracked open the top of his beer and poured it into the pint glass, though his gaze hadn't wandered much from her face. "I'm sure you know how lonely it can get when on a job away from home."

"Yeah…" Wasn't she suffering from the same fate? She sat down across from him.

And just like that, her thoughts went to Conall, desperate to have him back.

CHAPTER Eight

ITH HIS EYES racing over the lines of code, Conall wondered if he'd find what caused the power surge at Maggie's beast of a bus. It hadn't taken him long to regret leaving her on her own, and he was now desperately looking for a distraction. If not, there was a good chance he'd find himself racing back to her side to try to convince her he'd be worthy company for the night.

There was nothing in the code, which meant it was outside interference, either a normally occurring surge that somehow managed to overpower the system or a device used to temporarily fry the connection. He should tell her. She'd want to know. Not that it couldn't wait until morning. But if it was the latter and someone tripped the alarm, then she needed to be aware of it.

And it had nothing to do with the fact that he couldn't stop thinking of her. Damn it. How could he not after kissing her, touching her, seeing her half-naked? Hell, he wouldn't be a guy if he didn't still want her. The mere of thought of her had him going hard again. It was enough to have him grabbing his keys and heading out the door to see if they could pick up where they'd left off.

There wasn't a moment's hesitation, his focus complete on the only thing that mattered in that moment. Maggie. It didn't matter that she might think him crazy. Or that he didn't want anything serious. Nor did he care that she might turn him away yet again. He just had to see her. Had to feel her lush lips on his, her curves against his body, the weight of her breast in his palm, the warmth of her in his lap.

Occupied as he was with his thoughts, the drive was at once a blur while also lasting an eternity, taking him far too long to reach his destination. All he wanted was to be by her side. He thought of how he'd pull her into his arms the moment he got there. Kiss her. Hold her. Thought of how her breath would catch when he ran his hands down her back and nuzzled her, his stubble grazing the smooth skin of her neck as he nipped his way down the slope of her shoulder.

He pulled up to the church and threw the car in park, a glow seeping out through the windshield of the bus and into the dark of night. He took a deep breath and a moment to calm himself before heading to her door and knocking. It took longer than he'd expected for her to answer, but knew she'd likely be checking her security monitors and overriding the systems before letting him in.

The door opened, leaving her silhouetted in light. "Conall...what's wrong?"

"Nothing, lass." He climbed the few steps between them, and wrapped an arm around her waist, covering her mouth with his, taking, tasting. Her eyes went wide, not having expected it, her body stiff, but only for a moment before going supple under his touch, though she still tried to hold him at bay, her hands on his chest.

And then he knew why. "Maggie, is everything all right?"

Conall pulled away, anger and jealousy balling up in his gut as he spotted Andrew. His hands curled into tight fists, his chest so tight he could barely breathe. It was like his past coming back to haunt him, his scars torn open. He turned a hard gaze on Maggie. "Ye want to tell me what's going on here, Maggie?"

"Not particularly—though I can tell ye, it's not what ye think." She crossed her arms in front of her chest.

"The lady's allowed to choose the company she wants to keep." Andrew's smug smile had Conall moving forward to pummel the bastard, though Maggie held Conall back with a firm hand to his chest and another wrapped tightly around his arm.

She glanced over her shoulder. "Andrew, I think it's best ye go."

Conall headed down the few steps and back into the open so Andrew could pass, though Maggie kept a hold of his arm as if to keep him from lunging at Andrew.

What the hell had he been thinking to fall for her? Because that was exactly what had happened. Like a fool, he'd let her into his life when he knew better than to let his guard down.

"I'll see you tomorrow, *love*." The way Andrew's gaze lingered on her had Conall's fists clenching tight again.

"Just go, Andrew—and it's Maggie to you." Maggie threw him a baleful glare, and then once it was just the two of them, she took Conall's hand and led him back onto the bus. "Come on."

Although Conall was still furious, in part with himself for being stupid enough to let her into his life, he followed behind her. She put a glass of beer in the sink—probably Andrew's—and then turned with a sigh, leaning against the counter, her arms crossed in front of her chest once more. "Ye know I can do as I please at this point in our relationship. Until we establish some sort of commitment level, I'm a free agent."

He wanted to groan. Of course she was right. So why was it the woman made him crazy? "I know that."

"That said, *nothing* was going on with Andrew. He showed up and sort of finagled his way in for a drink."

"No offense, lass, but ye don't exactly seem the sort to let anyone *finagle* anything unless ye want them to." The heat in his gut—his anger, jealousy, frustration and the pent-up passion that had him driving to her in the first place—left him wanting to take her then and there, to claim her as his own.

"He guilted me into being hospitable—which is the same reason I haven't tossed ye out of here on yer arse for pulling this attitude with me. I like ye, Conall. A lot. Hell…" She shook her head. "Probably more than is wise. But I'll not suffer through your alpha male shite. I'm not yours, Conall."

His jaw was set tight, his body tense. "Not yet, anyway." He all but growled at the thought of her with another.

She started to say something, but he was having none of it. He now had one goal in mind, and one goal only. With an arm around her waist, he silenced her words with a hard kiss, his mouth bullying hers, her resistance fleeting as she now returned his passions. She was yanking off his jacket as his hands slipped onto the warm skin of her waist, pulling her shirt up and over her head, their kisses stopping no longer than necessary. A flick of the clasp and her bra soon found its way to the floor, with his shirt adding to the pile.

By the gods, he'd never wanted anyone more and she left his head dizzy and heart yearning. All logic, all thought, all caution melted in her touch, her kiss, the feel of her body yielding to him. She was all that mattered, all he needed—and he'd be damned if he was going to share her with another.

He spun her around to face the counter, and pressed himself against her from behind, as one hand fisted her hair and pulled her head back so he could feast on the soft curve of her neck, while his other hand cupped her perfect breast. A whimper of need escaped her lips as he toyed with her hard nipples and she ground her hips against his hard length, his heart thrashing against his ribs.

"Bed." It was all he could manage to get out, reduced to a monosyllabic vocabulary by his need for her. He'd take her against the counter if they waited any longer.

She spun in his arms, their kisses deepening as she moved them towards the back of the bus and through a narrow doorway, a bed just beyond. The way she looked at him, her eyes alight as she bit her lip and the way her hair cascaded over naked breasts, had his erection growing up past the edge of his jeans. Nearly all self-control was lost when she freed him, her hand running over the taut skin, making it pulse under her touch. With her help, he rid himself of his jeans and then yanked hers off, taking her black lace panties with them.

Bloody hell, she was beautiful. And just like that, he felt his heart slip another notch down that slippery slope of no return. Not that he cared. At that very moment, he'd give her anything she wanted—including his heart.

Taking a moment to steady himself, he brushed the hair from her eyes, his touch lingering before leaning in to kiss her. "Ye're mine, Maggie. If we're to do this, there's to be no other. Are we clear? I'll not share ye. Not with Andrew. Not with anyone."

She laughed and kissed him again. "Aye, love. I'm yours and no other's."

How Conall managed to get anything done over the next few days was beyond him. He'd been working right alongside Maggie, each of them doing their thing and collaborating when need be. They'd then spend the evening in each other's company, and their nights tangled in each other's arms.

He looked over at her as she tinkered with one of her contraptions, and thought her the most seductive and intelligent creature he'd ever seen.

She was unlike any other woman he'd dated—and certainly nothing like Janet who'd broken his heart repeatedly and made him swear off any and all serious relationships. Yet being with Maggie was enough to have him rethinking his stance, suddenly willing to risk heartache if it meant he could be with her.

It surprised him that he could fall for her so hard and fast. And even more surprising was that he was willing to put his heart on the line. How could he hold back when she gave him everything she had? The girl did nothing in half-measures. Not with her work, and not with her affections. Better yet, with them openly pursuing a relationship, Andrew was finally keeping his distance.

Conall wasn't normally the jealous sort but Maggie brought out something fierce and primal in him—not to mention his protective side. And it wasn't that he didn't trust her—he did—but he sure as hell didn't trust Andrew. The man irked him like few others, especially when he'd been so intent on pursuing her.

With his laptop and equipment slung over his shoulder, he headed out to his car, where it was parked next to Maggie's bus. He tossed the stuff in the back seat while thinking of their plans for the evening when he spotted her walking towards him. She looked around as if to make sure they were alone, and then leapt into his arms as he spun her around to absorb her momentum, her legs wrapped around his waist and her arms around his neck.

"Where are *you* sneaking off to?" Maggie's smile slipped towards the mischievous, her eyes bright with humor. His body's reaction to having her in his arms was instantaneous, and it took all he had to not press her against the hood of his car and set off his car alarm. "You must know I have plans for ye. All day long, you've looked far too enticing."

"Enticing, eh?" He had to laugh. She lowered her legs to the ground, though she'd yet to step out of his arms. "Ye're the only one who could think I'm enticing when I've done nothing more than sit in front of a computer screen all day."

"And ye're damn lucky I do, Mr. Stewart. This way we can skip right to the fun stuff, and ye need not woo me." She flicked her eyebrows up and gave him a seductive look over her shoulder as she wandered to her bus. "Are ye not coming then? It's not nice to keep a lady waiting."

"Maggie…" He grabbed her hand to stop her from going any further. It was an idea he'd been toying with but had dismissed it as too soon. Yet now it felt like perfect timing. "Since it's Friday, and we have the weekend ahead of us, I thought we might go away for a day or two. What do ye say? Rowan and Angus agreed to take Piper."

Her eyes widened in surprise, a crooked smile tugging at her lips as she wandered back into his embrace. With her arms slipping around his neck, she trailed kisses across his jawline to his ear, her words spoken between nips, which had him going even harder. "What did ye have in mind, lover?"

Lover…that word left him dizzy. "London, Edinburgh, Paris…wherever ye'd like to go." It didn't matter where they ended up, as long as he could get her naked.

"Dublin. I want to show ye around my ole stomping ground. And I want to check in with me parents. I've been gone a while. Ye don't mind, do ye? We wouldn't stay with them, or anything that extreme." She wrapped her arms around his neck and kissed him—kissed him until he'd agree to anything she wanted. "Please? I promise I'll more than make it up to ye."

"Aye, love. Whate'er makes ye happy."

Bloody hell. He was going to be meeting her parents. Not exactly what he'd had in mind—and yet he didn't care, nor did he mind, as long as she was in his arms.

She went on her tippy toes and bit his lip. "*You* do. *You* make me happy—like no one else ever has."

They'd landed and booked a room in the center of Dublin, but before they'd even had the chance to unpack, she'd rented a motorbike and had them on their way to Blackrock. He'd held onto her for dear life as she sped through traffic, leaving him to wonder how she'd managed to live this long. By the time they got to her parents' house, his legs were wobbly as custard on a hot day—though he couldn't blame the ride entirely.

It didn't matter that this was a simple visit to see her parents because she happened to be in town. Meeting the parents always increased the seriousness of a relationship. It was a big step, and one he'd only done once before. To do this now with Maggie…it left his stomach in knots.

"Are ye sure it's a good idea to surprise yer family? With me in tow? I'm sure they'd rather have ye all to themselves." Conall seldom cared what anyone thought of him, but this was different. This was Maggie's family. And he couldn't imagine they'd be happy about their only daughter shacking up with someone she'd known barely a month, even if they'd be sharing a hotel room for no more than the weekend. "Ye're their wee lass and ye have a gaggle of brothers."

"You're worrying too much. They'll like ye just fine." She took his hand and pulled him towards the door, walking backwards.

"Ye forget I've got a sister of my own, and I can tell ye now, yer brothers and father are *not* going to be happy." He was doomed. But one look from Maggie and he knew he'd do just about anything for her. The feelings she elicited in him had gone far beyond the physical. And though that scared him to no end, he couldn't imagine it being any other way.

"Liam's the worst of them, and he's away on that job. Ye have nothing to worry about." She leaned over and gave him a peck before ringing the doorbell. "And I promise to make it up to ye once we're back at the hotel."

"Are ye sure ye don't want to head back now?" She didn't get a chance to answer him, and he didn't get a chance to escape. The door was pulled open by a young man in his early twenties, who was no doubt her brother with his thick golden brown hair, ice blue eyes, and athletic build. Probably Patrick, if he recalled Maggie's rundown of her family correctly.

"Maggie…ye should have called." He caught his sister in a big hug, while giving Conall the crook eye.

Bloody hell. This was going to be a long day.

CHAPTER
Nine

MAGGIE FELT BAD. Sort of. Actually, it was hard not to find the whole thing humorous—not that Conall shared her sentiment if his stiff shoulders were anything to go by. The poor man looked like he was navigating a minefield as he sat across from her father and two brothers, Aidan and Patrick.

Her da sat forward with a hard gaze pinned on Conall, his ice blue eyes so similar to her own. He looked good for a man in his late fifties, still bearing an athletic build, even if he'd gotten leaner in more recent years and his brown hair was now liberally streaked with grey. "Computer security? And how does that work when ye're up in the middle of nowhere?"

Her two brothers mumbled something to each other, too low for anyone else to hear, and then laughed, making Maggie want to lean over and smack their heads together.

Conall shrugged at her father's question, not rising to the bait. "Most of my work is done remotely, and if need be, I travel. It seems not to be an issue for my clients, many of which are in Scotland."

"And ye think ye'll be able to make my Maggie happy? She's a city girl, born and bred, *laddie.*" Her da scoffed as Maggie threw him a glare, silently begging him not to do this. Conall was skittish enough about relationships without her father making matters worse.

"Honestly? I've always believed that the person ye're with matters more than the setting. I like Maggie—a lot. But only she knows what will make her happy. I can only try my best to do right by her." Conall reached over and took her hand, giving her a small smile that made her heart race. He then locked eyes with her father. "And I'm smart enough to know that she makes her own decisions. She won't stay anywhere or with anyone if she doesn't want to."

She loved that Conall wasn't backing down. Most men forced to confront her father would either be quaking in their boots or would have already abandoned the cause and headed for the door. Her da knew it, too, and though most couldn't read the signs, it was clear he liked Conall—as much as he'd ever like someone she was seeing.

"Quit harassing him, Da." She gave her father a teasing smile, before nestling against Conall's side. "We've only been together a few weeks, and ye're grilling him like he's going to ask for my hand in marriage."

"Well, love, what else am I to think when the two of ye are going to be holed up in some hotel in the city?" Her father shook his head, his body stiff. "I know ye're an adult and ye make yer own choices, but ye're still my little girl and ye're daft if ye think I'll be happy about it. Just be grateful these are modern times and we don't already have him hogtied and heading for the church."

"*Da!*"

Keys jingled in the front door and her mother walked in, saving Maggie and Conall from further interrogation and a quickie wedding. Maggie was already heading over to greet her ma.

"*Maggie*. Ye should have said ye were coming." Her mother pulled her into a tight hug and kissed her cheek. It didn't take long for her ma to spot Conall or her father and brothers just beyond. "I'm Nora. Have the boys been behaving themselves?"

Maggie crossed her arms in front of her chest and with a smug smile, glared at the male members of her family. "Of course not. They've all but raked Conall over hot coals."

Conall stood and shook her mother's hand. "It's a pleasure to meet ye."

Her ma gave him an easy smile. "The pleasure's mine. I hope ye'll stay for lunch."

Maggie linked her fingers with Conall's, a smile dancing on her lips as she looked up at him, utterly and completely smitten. "Aye, Ma. That would be perfect."

Aidan shifted his gaze from her to Conall and then back again. "Maggie…could I have a word?"

She gave Conall's hand a squeeze to keep him from worrying, though she didn't know how he'd fare alone with her parents and remaining brother. "I'll be but a minute."

Narrowing her eyes at her younger brother, she followed him out to their backyard. She'd be more than a little annoyed if he was pulling her aside for a lecture on her relations with Conall, even if he was just being protective. "What's this about, Aidan?"

"I don't want to go worrying ye, but I thought ye should know. Seamus Flaherty ran into Da at the pub and was asking about you and your work." He ran a rough hand across his chin. "Ye know what Flaherty's like, aye? Figured ye might want to keep an eye out."

She groaned. This was trouble she didn't need. Few knew that her father spent his formative years as a thief—a damn good one, too, until he met her ma, fell in love and abandoned his old life for one on the straight and narrow. Not exactly the sort of information she wanted getting out when she ran a security firm—even if her father was a big part of why she was so good at her job. And what the hell would Conall think when he also dealt with company securities? It certainly wouldn't do his reputation any good either.

Unfortunately, Flaherty ran the crew her da had been with and had yet to abandon his career for more honorable and legal pursuits. "Did Da mention the Hope—the necklace?"

"No, but I imagine Flaherty already knew about it if he was asking after ye." Aidan tugged at one of her loose locks, as if hearkening back to the days when he was just a wee lad and used to pull her hair. "Ye'll be careful, yeah?"

"Yeah." She looked at her little brother, all grown up and worrying about her. It was hard to be away for so long, always on a job. Seemed he'd become a man when she had her back turned. "The Flaherty crew is always snooping around, but it seldom amounts to much. They usually have enough to keep them busy without pissing on their home turf. And they know not to anger Da. Still…with a big enough prize, they might risk it, and the Highlander's Hope is certainly that. Don't go worrying about it too much, though."

"I'll keep an eye out and an ear to the ground. If I hear of anything more, I'll be sure to send word." Aidan stuck his hands in his pockets, his brow still furrowed with worry.

"I appreciate it. And don't go worrying yerself. It'll be fine." She reached up and ruffled his thick hair, just like she used to when he was little.

"By the way, I like yer fella there. Doesn't say much, but seems like he'll do right by ye." He gave her a crooked smile. "Though I hope ye realize, it'd be a hell of a lot easier on us if every guy didn't go falling in love with ye."

She burst out laughing. "As if that's ever been the case, ye wee gobshite."

"Thanks for doing that, love." Maggie mumbled the words between kisses, as Conall leaned against the hotel door, pushing it shut. All morning long she'd been looking forward to getting him alone.

"Och, ye'll be making it up to me, lass." Conall laughed against her lips as his hands slipped under her shirt, hot against her skin, his touch making her heart race. "I thought they might take me out back and string me up by my ankles for having the audacity to seek yer company."

She smiled between kisses. "They liked ye."

"Bloody hell. I'd hate to see what they're like when they *don't* like one of yer boyfriends." Trailing slow kisses down her neck, they moved farther into the room while she tugged at his sweater, desperate to get the man naked.

He was so unlike anyone she knew, let alone dated, and despite his brusque exterior, he left her breathless now that he'd let his guard down and she'd gotten to know him better. Each moment spent in his company, in his arms, left him claiming yet another piece of her heart. And she was happy to give it to him—except for the fact that he'd made it clear he had no interest in that sort of thing.

So what the hell was she doing? It was one thing to live her life to the fullest and another to foolishly risk her heart on someone who'd made his stance clear.

"What's wrong, love? Ye're distracted and yer smile's faded." He cupped her cheek in his hand, and brushed a thumb across her skin, his brow drawn with worry. "I was just teasing about yer family. Actually, they were rather entertaining, especially with yer mother there. And damn funny once they got started."

She managed a smile, not wanting him to worry. The poor man had been through enough without making him discuss their relationship. "I'm just happy ye didn't get scared off."

"Takes more than that, love. And family's important. I'd not have it any other way." His eyes were still taking her in, and she knew he wasn't wholly convinced. "So, why don't ye tell me what's really going on? I'm not some wee laddie, aye? I can handle it. And I don't want anything getting in the way of our weekend together. Is it something yer brother said?"

"No, love…" When he nuzzled her and gave her a sweet kiss, it gave her courage the boost it needed. "It's just that…you were never meant to be more than a bit of fun. A way to pass the time while on the job."

With pursed lips and his eyes narrowed, he wasn't looking happy. Not one bit. He pulled away from her and started to pace. "What are ye trying to tell me, Maggie? That none of this matters? That I'm just here to keep ye from getting bored?"

Bleedin' hell, he'd misinterpreted what she meant. "No, you fool. The exact opposite."

His pacing stopped and he turned towards her. Though he said nothing, she could see his jaw was still clenched tightly, despite his thick stubble.

She took his hand and moved to his side, a smile tugging at her lips. "I'm trying to tell you that I've fallen for ye. Stupidly, head over heels, fallen for ye."

"So what's the problem, Maggie?" He shook his head, still serious, as her smile faded and she was back to her original concerns.

"The problem is you've made it abundantly clear that ye have no interest in pursuing something serious. And that was perfectly fine when you were just a distraction." She leaned her head against his chest, unable to look at him. "I don't know when things changed or why, but they did and…I don't want to have my heart broken, Conall."

He lifted her chin up so she'd be forced to look at him. "I won't deny not wanting a relationship—and that sure as hell was the case when we first started. But Maggie…like you, I've had to rethink what I truly want. It doesn't escape me that we've not known each other long, but it seems not to matter." He brushed her lips with his in a whisper of a kiss that had her leaning into him.

He left her breathless. "What are ye saying?"

With a sigh, he nestled his cheek against hers, the scent of him intoxicating—like a winter sea laced with smoke and leather. "I'm saying that ye've turned my world upside down. I never wanted this, love. Yet now, there's nothing I want more than to be with ye. And I don't want this to be casual, Maggie. Nor do I want it to end in a few months when ye've moved on to the next job and town."

Her breath caught in her chest, as if she might scare him away by simply exhaling. He'd been so standoffish. And now? Was he really giving her—giving them—a chance? "It's a big step for ye, isn't it?"

"Aye, love. I'll not deny it. My parents didn't have an easy go of it, and I'm afraid my own experiences left me not wanting to pursue anything serious. But everything changed with you." He then laughed and brushed her cheek, mischief sparking in his eyes. "From the moment I first saw ye sticking out of that hole with yer arse in the air, I was a goner."

She slapped his chest playfully. "Ye're such a troublemaker."

"Me?" He shook his head, some of his smile fading. "If anyone's trouble, it's you, love. Ye'll likely shatter my heart to pieces, yet I'm helpless to walk away."

His words were like a vice around her heart. She hadn't realized until that very moment how badly he'd been hurt. He was taking a leap of faith—with her. It wasn't just a big step. It was huge. And in that moment, she felt her heart slip that final notch.

She cupped his face in her hands, searched his eyes, her heart overflowing, her chest tight with emotion. "I love ye, Conall. I don't know when it happened or how, but it did. And I swear I'll not hurt ye."

His gaze trailed over her face as if searching for the truth in her words. He brushed the hair from her eyes, and then kissed her, slowly, sweetly, as if they were the only two people in the world. It didn't matter that he hadn't spoken the words in return, not when she could read his emotions so easily in his touch, his kiss.

She lost herself in him, left to wonder how he could claim her heart in so little time, yet no longer able to imagine her life without him in it. What she felt, how he made her feel…it didn't matter that they'd not known each other long.

When his kisses slowed, he still held her close, cradling her against him. "By the gods, Maggie…this isn't what I expected or wanted."

She pulled out of his arms, confused and starting to feel like a fool. She should have kept her mouth shut. "Well then, I'm sorry for putting ye in such an awkward position."

"Och, love, that's not what I meant." He shook his head with a laugh and blocked her slap to the chest. "Bloody hell, woman, ye have a wee temper, don't ye? I'm trying to tell ye that I hadn't expected to fall in love with ye."

Her heart hitched to hear him say he loved her, not quite believing it. "Are ye sure that's what it is?"

He shrugged, his face blank. "Either that or it's the airline food giving me indigestion."

She burst out laughing as he pulled her into his arms, her heart ready to burst with happiness.

"I love ye, Maggie Brennan. Gods help me."

CHAPTER
Ten

A FTER LEAVING THE hotel for a bite to eat, Conall let Maggie show him around the city. Not that he hadn't been to Dublin before, but this was *her* Dublin. Pubs that had been around hundreds of years, hole-in-the-wall eateries to sop up the drink between stops, and dingy used record shops. With luck, they'd still manage to crawl back to their hotel room—if they could find it.

Conall wandered behind Maggie as she dragged him into a music shop. Most of it was sectioned off to house used albums, with the remaining space used to display a wide variety of instruments, some new, most used. "Another one of yer hangouts?"

"Yeah…used to spend my paychecks here when I was in school. Could never resist. Wish I could play, but never had the patience to learn." She flicked through a few albums, and threw him a sideways glance. "The guitar at your place—have you been playing long?"

He tensed at the mention of it. "Aye. Though I don't play much anymore." He really didn't want to have to explain how he'd lost all desire to play during his troubles with Janet. And now? Playing it only reminded him of how happy he'd once been. Before he'd gotten his heart trounced on.

She grabbed his hand and looked up at him with a flirty pout. "Ye have to play for me once we get back. Please…"

He didn't want to ruin the great evening they'd been having, but he wouldn't make a promise he couldn't keep, either. He let out a weary sigh. "Nae, love. I can't."

Her smile faded. "Oh…"

"Maggie, I'm sorry. It's just…complicated. It has nothing to do with you, love." He cupped her cheek and pulled her close for a kiss. "Can ye forgive me?"

He saw her struggle, but only for a minute more, a smile forcing its way to her lips. "There's nothing to forgive. Ready for the next stop on our tour?"

By the gods, he was one lucky man. "That I am, love."

With their arms wrapped around each other, they made their way to a pub Maggie used to frequent. And damn if that woman wasn't going to drink him under the table. Sitting at the bar, Conall nursed his pint with Maggie tucked in at his side, this crowded pub just one of many Maggie had dragged him to.

"How do ye do it, lass? I must be getting old." It's not that they were necessarily having a lot to drink, but it'd been years since he had more than a pint or two.

"Ye can't *not* go drinking with the lads in this industry. It's bad enough I'm a woman, aye?" She ran a hand down his thigh while taking another pull of her pint.

"There's nothing bad about it from where I'm standing." He leaned over and nuzzled her, unable to stay away for long. She was so beautiful, so alive, it stole his breath.

He still couldn't quite believe how things had turned out between them. He hadn't expected to ever fall for anyone again, knowing the risks were too great and not worth the hassle. Instead he'd fallen harder and faster for Maggie than he could have ever imagined falling for anyone. She'd leave him shattered if she ever broke things off between them. And he didn't think he'd ever recover.

He kissed her as if she alone could sustain him, his head dizzy with the feel of her in his arms, her sweet scent drawing him in. "Let's head back, love."

She nipped at his bottom lip and pulled him close, her arms wrapped around his waist. "Sounds perfect."

"Little Maggie Brennan. Been a long time."

Conall turned to find a man in his late twenties looking at the two of them, Maggie stiff in his arms. She straightened up and cocked her head. "Sean Flaherty."

"Are ye not going to introduce me to your fella?" He flicked a look at Conall, but his gaze didn't stray from Maggie long. It made Conall's back go up.

"We were just leaving." Maggie was already shrugging into her jacket and then grabbed Conall's hand. "Are ye ready, love?"

"Aye." Conall didn't know how well Maggie and Sean knew each other. Nor did he know their history. However, it was clear she didn't like the man, and he was happy to take his cue from her.

"Sorry to see ye go so soon, Maggie."

But she was already heading through the crowd, not bothering to look back at Sean or acknowledge him further. By the time they made it out onto the street, her pace was brisk and she was in one hell of a mood.

"Maggie…" She slowed a bit, turning to face him. Conall didn't want to pry, but if Sean was trouble, he'd like to know. "Do ye want to tell me what that was about?"

"No. Not really." She continued down the road when Conall slowed to a stop, forcing her to do the same, their hands still linked.

"We're together now, aye?" He brushed her cheek. "And I'm not trying to pry—yer business is still yer own. But Maggie...I don't like to be left in the dark, especially if someone's been giving ye a hard time."

"It's nothing, love. I swear." Though she cupped his cheek and kissed him, her lips lingering on his, there was a tension in her body that had yet to ease—and that left him worried. "He's not important and it's been over a year since I last saw him."

Something still felt off—and he wasn't blind. "Were ye lovers in the past?"

She sighed. "He's the son of one of me da's colleagues."

He shook his head and stepped away, knowing she wasn't being completely honest with him. "I'd appreciate the truth, Maggie. It's not like either of us was the Virgin Mary before this, and I get that ye won't always be able to tell me everything, but I won't tolerate lies or half-truths."

"Ye're right, and I'm sorry. It's not like it's a big deal." She sighed. "I did see him for a short while, but it was ages ago when I was young and stupid. It was never anything serious—no more than a summer fling—and I rarely see him anymore, except by chance."

Some of the tension in his shoulders eased. She'd told him the truth, and though he'd prefer to not have to prod her into it, he'd only needed to ask once. "I appreciate yer honesty."

"I'm just not used to discussing my past. I try to keep my focus on the present and the future." She shook her head, her smile long gone. "It's not always easy to do, ye know."

So unlike her bubbly self, he pulled her into his arms to comfort her. Maybe he wasn't the only one with a painful history. "I don't want to be dredging things up for ye, love. We both have pasts, aye? But I don't want things to feel superficial between us. I'll say it again—I love ye, Maggie." By the gods, it sent a pulse of fear and excitement through him to speak those words.

"And I love you, Conall. Don't doubt it for a moment, for those aren't words I speak lightly." She fisted her hands in his jacket and pulled him near for a kiss, her lips tasting like honey and hops.

He brushed her hair from her eyes as the wind pulled it free, his touch lingering, the need to feel her close all-consuming. "Whatever's in yer past won't change the way I feel about ye. Ye don't need to rehash everything ye've ever been through, but know that I'm here for ye. Don't ever feel like ye can't speak to me about something, no matter what it is. I'll always be here for ye, love."

"And ye'll do the same?" Her eyes searched his, and for a moment, as he lost himself in those icy blue waters, it felt like their souls were linked.

"Aye, love. I will." He wished he could kiss her worries away.

"So, then…the guitar? Don't tell me there's nothing to it." With her ice blue eyes locked on his, he knew there'd be no avoiding the matter. And it was only fair that he now fess up to a part of his past.

"I used to play all the time, but after Janet…I don't know. It was sort of like I lost that part of me." Wrapping his arms around her, he held her close, leaning his cheek atop her head. "Maybe someday, aye?"

"Let's head back to the hotel. I don't want there to be any secrets between us. I'll tell ye everything there is to know if you'll do the same." She looked up at him, her brow furrowed as if waiting for him to protest.

He found himself fighting back a flare of panic, but pushed his worries aside, knowing they had to do this. Neither of them could back down without leaving the other hurt or making them think they were hiding something. And given how quickly they'd fallen for each other, it would do them good to get to know each other better. Still…the whole thing had his muscles in knots, especially since he'd never really discussed his past relationships with anyone.

With her tucked in at her side, they wandered down the road and made their way back to their room, his mind still racing over what he'd tell her and how.

He locked the door behind them, the beat of his heart stuttering. He'd gone and dug himself one hell of a deep hole, and had little chance of getting out of it. At least she was right there with him in the same big hole and no doubt just as nervous.

Needing to feel her touch, he pulled her into his arms and then laughed at how on edge she'd made him. "Maybe we don't need to do this."

"Are ye wimping out on me, Conall?" She kissed the hollow of his neck, making him want to ditch talking and get her naked. "We can tackle the hard stuff tonight, like relationships. The rest of it—crazy nights, drunken escapades and college stunts—can wait for another day."

Conall groaned, unable to ignore his growing need for her. "Can't we leave the chatting 'til later?" Her hand slipped down his chest and continued south. "Bloody hell, woman. I won't be able to put a coherent thought together if ye keep that up."

"Might be fun to chat while getting naked. That way, we can easily distract each other if things start to feel too serious." She bit his nipple through the fabric of his shirt, his self-control slipping another notch.

"That's it." He could take no more. No longer capable of thought, he picked her up and carried her off to the bed as she squealed with laughter. She was already wriggling out of her tight jeans while he made quick work of his own clothing, discarding them in a hurried heap before nestling himself between her naked legs. He nipped at her nipple and then trailed kisses down her side, murmuring against her soft skin. "By all means, feel free to start hashing out yer past."

With a squeal, she pushed him away. "Okay, stop. I can't concentrate when ye're kissing me like that."

"Ye recall, this was yer idea, aye?" He had to laugh. It was no wonder she left him dizzy.

She smiled apologetically, and pulled him towards her, giving him a quick kiss on the lips. "Sorry…I swear I'll make it up to ye afterwards. And I don't know about you, but I won't take long. The last thing I want to do is linger on this topic."

"No worries, aye? Take however long ye need." Doing what he could to ignore his aching need, he grabbed the throw from the bottom of the bed and pulled her into his arms, kissing the top of her head. "I'm listening, love."

"If we're talking about relationships, it's nothing more than the usual. Dated a bunch when I was younger and while at university, before things got pretty serious with this one guy. Oliver. We were together years, yeah? He was smart, funny—great in bed—and could be so sweet." She shrugged, her fingers absent-mindedly playing with the fringe on the blanket as he tried not to picture her naked in another man's arms. "We were young. I get that. But I gave him everything. My entire heart. I held nothing back. Unfortunately…"

Conall sighed, her story too familiar. "You were the only one giving fully."

"And I was clueless. Didn't realize it until he broke things off. Like I said, it's not any different from every other breakup story, but it really caught me off guard. If there were signs, I hadn't seen them. And I took it hard. Spent months in a hopeless darkness, severely depressed, and I swear it felt like I'd never escape it." She let out a long, weary breath. "By the time I managed to pull myself free of it, I promised myself I'd not waste another day—and if I gave my heart to anyone again, they best be willing to reciprocate fully. I don't do anything by halves, Conall."

"Aye, love. I wouldn't expect ye to." He kissed her, now understanding her so much better. "It's why ye always say ye live life to the fullest, aye?"

"Yeah…when I finally came around, I realized I'd wasted nearly a year of my life. A year I wouldn't get back. I've dated plenty since then, but… this…what we have feels different." She looked up at him, worry lining her face. "I need to know ye'll not hold back, Conall."

"How could I hold back when ye've shown me what it is to truly love someone—and to be truly loved?" He kissed her, and then steeling himself, got ready to tell her his story. "I'll tell ye now, my story's not much different from yer own. Dated a bit, got to college and fell for someone there. Janet. Broke my heart. Then came back begging for forgiveness and I took her back only to have her break my heart again. I know, I was a fool to think she'd changed and that lying and cheating on me was just a one-off. But that sort of thing never is, is it? I left for the States to get away from her and go to grad school."

He hated having to think about it, and his mood had now soured. Until Maggie held him tightly. "I swear, Conall, I'll only ever tell ye the truth. You can trust me, love."

He kissed her, and with it went the hurt he'd been keeping balled up all those years. "I already do."

"Just look at you." Rowan was grinning ear to ear. "You're...*happy*. I swear, I never thought I'd see the day. That must have been some trip to Dublin. Has Lara seen you like this? She'll probably drop dead right there on the spot, ale and burgers all over the floor."

Angus pulled her away, and nestled her against his side, silencing her with a quick kiss. "Quit harassing the poor man. Ye'll make him self-conscious and then we'll get the old scowling Conall back."

Conall leaned back against the counter, his smile refusing to be contained. "Tease all ye want. Just remember, I know what the two of ye were like when ye first started dating and were mooning o'er each other—not that it's changed any."

"So, when are we going to have you and Maggie over for dinner?" Rowan's eyes sparked with mischief and a grin tugged at her lips. "Maybe I should steal her for a girls' night out first. That way I can get all the juicy details about Dublin beforehand."

"I swear, lass, ye're nothing but trouble." Conall shook his head, thinking he should have snuck in to get Piper when they were away at work so he could spare himself Rowan's inquisition and teasing.

"Did ye meet her family then?" Even Angus was looking curious.

He sighed, knowing it'd be near impossible to avoid discussing the details. Not that he really wanted to keep things from them. Rowan and Angus had become good friends, and he valued their friendship. "Aye, I did. Both her parents and her two brothers. The third brother's the one who works with her. Been away on some other job they've got going."

Angus scoffed out a laugh. "And ye made it back in one piece? They must have liked ye, then."

Conall shrugged. "I sure as hell hope so."

Rowan's jaw dropped open and her eyes went wide, excitement thrumming through her. "No frigging way! *You're in love!*"

He must have blushed a thousand shades of red. Yet there was no hiding it, and he certainly wasn't going to deny it. Publicly acknowledging how he felt for Maggie was a huge step for him. Yet it felt right.

He ran a rough hand across his stubbled chin, a smile tugging at his lips. "Aye, I am. Well and truly a goner, I'm afraid."

Chapter Eleven

ANDREW WAS A nice enough guy, but Maggie swore he was on the jobsite just to get in her way and distract her from getting any work done. He kept wanting to chat and linger, and she had far too long a list she needed to finish if she had any hope of staying on schedule. Small problems with the job continued to pop up, making her wonder if the necklace had some sort of curse on it. Most of her jobs ran smoothly, but this one here hit one snag after another.

"How was Dublin? It's been ages since I last got over there." Andrew leaned against her worktable, his long legs stretched out in front of him as she soldered her connections.

"It was fine." The man must be blind if he didn't see that she wasn't in the mood for conversation. Maybe if she were less subtle. "I'm really sorry, but I need to concentrate on getting this done so I can wrap up for the day."

"Yeah. Sure. Didn't mean to disrupt your work—and I probably should get back to mine. We're finishing up the main addition." He pushed away from her table and stuffed his hands in his jean pockets. "Don't suppose you'd be up for grabbing a pint, seeing as it's day's end?"

"Sorry. I've got plans with Conall." Andrew had to know she didn't go to Dublin alone. The man couldn't possibly be this dense. And Conall must have Andrew-ESP, since he was once more coming to save her. "Here he is now."

"I'll leave you to your work then." Andrew wandered off just as Conall approached.

Conall wrapped an arm around her waist, his gaze on Andrew until he was gone. Only then did he give her a quick kiss. "I swear I'm not the jealous sort, but that man makes me want to put a fist through his face."

"I don't know what to think of him anymore. I used to think he was just bored and interested, but he can't possibly be this determined or clueless." She snuggled closer to Conall, liking the feel of his solid comfort and the way he smelled of wood fire and the salty sea.

"Iain said they're nearly done with most of the construction. Hopefully that means Andrew will get sent to supervise a different job." He tilted his head towards the door. "Do ye have a minute? I was going over some of the data coming in off the security measures I have in place, and wanted yer opinion. I brought my laptop so ye won't have to head all the way back to my house. If we could use yer office, though, that'd be great."

"Yeah, sure." She quickly packed away her tools and headed for the bus, quickly overriding the security to let them in. Conall grabbed a seat and set up his laptop on the small table, the rest of the surfaces covered with her own equipment. Maggie looked over his shoulder at the information he was pulling up. "What do ye have?"

"Honestly, it could be nothing. But ye see here?" He pointed to a running list of data taken from the security checks run by his scanners. "This feels a bit off to me. Like someone was pinging our walls to test the threshold of what would trigger a reaction. What I need is to look at yer systems to see if there's anything similar."

Maggie pulled up a seat beside him and accessed her security systems. She was decent with computer stuff, but she didn't quite see the pattern Conall was finding in his data. "Here…take a look. It's just one more thing, yeah? I swear, I've never had so many problems with a job before. Just small stuff—loose connections, snagged cables, chewed up wires. But it's starting to take its toll on my deadlines."

"Old places like this can be like that, given the moisture and age of the place—not to mention the rodent population. Until it's sealed tight and the environmentals are running, I'd imagine ye'll still hit a few snags." He tilted his head towards the screen. "Let me see what ye've got."

She slid over so he could take a look, his eyes already scanning the information. He worked quickly, keying through the information, his focus complete. And she had to admit, it was a complete turn-on to see him work. Not only was he ruggedly gorgeous, he was brilliant—and that was like catnip to her. He was absolutely irresistible.

"I don't know. It's not really anything conclusive, but I do want to keep an eye on it. I'll throw up additional precautions and monitoring for the entire system." He let out a sigh, and then spun to face her. "Don't suppose I can interest ye in dinner?"

"That all depends on what ye're offering for dessert." She flicked her eyebrows up with a teasing smile, not sure she'd ever get her fill of him.

He pulled her close and kissed her until she was breathless, her head spinning and her body thrumming with need. She got to her feet and pulled her t-shirt up over her head, eliciting a smile from him. "Dessert first, I take it?"

She shrugged with a flirty look and wandered towards the bedroom in the back of the bus. "Life's too short to wait until after dinner."

Conall certainly didn't need a lot of encouragement, his lips already on hers as his hands wandered over her skin. Still kissing him, she made her way onto the bed, ridding him of his shirt so she could glimpse his hard abs in the moment before he covered her with his body. His scent filled her head as he trailed kisses over her face, leaving her desperate to have him once more.

"*Maggie!* For fuck's sake."

Bollocks! She scrambled to get her shirt on, grateful that Conall had been in the way and her brother had already disappeared back into the other room. Conall silently groaned, his eyes rolling upward. Once they were both dressed, Conall took her hand, kissed her quickly, and then led her into the living area of the bus.

"I'm Conall." He extended his hand and Liam hesitated a moment before shaking it.

"Liam—*her brother.*" Those last words were spoken through a clenched jaw as Liam scowled at the two of them. But Maggie was having none of it.

"Ye could have called to let me know you were coming." It wasn't the ideal situation, but he had no right to get angry. "And you can leave yer attitude at the door. I'm an adult—not some teenager. I make my own decisions and do as I wish, Liam. You should know that by now."

"As if I could forget." He shifted his gaze to Conall. "And you—do ye really think ye're up to the challenge of dealing with our sweet Maggie?"

Conall shrugged and threw her a smile. "I'll try my best, at any rate."

"Yeah…good luck with that." Her brother scoffed, still glaring at them. With arms crossed and a final shake of his head as if realizing there was nothing he could do, he gave up. "So, any decent place around here to get a bite and a pint? It feels like we're in the middle of fecking nowhere."

Maggie gave him a smile, happy to have her brother back, despite his surprise arrival and his rocky introduction to Conall. "Come on then. We'll show ye where the pub is. Introduce ye to the barkeep. Though ye'll want to stay in her good graces so she doesn't bar ye. Not many other places to go."

Liam gave her a crooked smile filled with mischief. "I'll keep that in mind."

Conall drove them into Dunmuir, the center of town quaint and picturesque with its pastel-colored shops facing the tiny fishing port, the setting sun painting the sky in pinks and oranges. Maggie pulled her jacket closed against the bitter wind coming in off the ocean as they walked to the pub, when Conall nestled her against his side with an arm around her, helping to keep her warm. Dublin could get cold, but it was nothing compared to the Scottish highlands.

Luckily, the pub was toasty warm with a nice fire going in the hearth, their table close enough to feel the warmth from the dancing flames. It didn't take long for Lara to show up with menus, but Maggie wasn't expecting the scowl on her face—especially not when it was directed at her brother.

"Ye have some nerve walking into my pub." She whacked Liam's shoulder with the menus, threw them down on the table and stormed off behind the bar.

Maggie turned to her brother, eyebrows perked in question. "Well, that was quick, even for you. What the hell did ye do to her?"

Liam groaned and rolled his eyes, looking miserable. "We hooked up when she was helping at her aunt's pub a few years ago—back when we were working in Falkirk. I'd meant to keep in touch, but lost her number after we moved on to the next job." He glanced in Lara's direction with a sigh, and ran his hand through his thick brown hair. "If ye'll excuse me a minute."

Maggie could easily believe he'd lost Lara's number. Her brother might be organized and reliable when it came to their work, but it didn't always carry over to the rest of his life, even if he meant well. "I'd like to see him sweet talk his way out of this one. Lara doesn't seem the forgiving type."

Conall scoffed with a half laugh. "No, she's not. And she's a smart lass, too, so I doubt he'll get away with much."

Maggie shrugged, throwing a glance over her shoulder to see how her brother was faring. "It'll do Liam some good if he can't use his charms. It's too easy for him to smile and flirt his way out of trouble, and I like

Lara. I hope she gives him a good tongue-lashing—especially if she wants to keep him interested."

Conall pulled her into his arms, the feel of him comforting. "Always thought it a waste that Lara came back after culinary school. I know her da needs the help and she's good with the running of the business, but most days, she's not doing much but waiting tables and pulling pints. Her father hasn't let her make any changes to the menu other than the specials. I think that's why she's such a pain in the arse—it's got to be frustrating for her, I'd imagine."

"So, why did *you* come back after school? I imagine it'd be easier for business if you were closer to a city." It's not like the highlands were a hotbed of computer activity. Hell, she was lucky if she could get cell phone reception in some spots.

Conall leaned in and kissed her cheek, his strong arm draped over her shoulder. It took another moment, which made her think he didn't discuss his private life much. "My father's on his own now that my parents have divorced and my sister's moved away. He's still young enough, but I don't like the thought of him being here with no one else around. Besides, the oil companies that work off the coast not far from here were some of my first big clients."

"So it made sense to stay local. Can't say I blame ye. The area's gorgeous." Craggy cliffs overlooking the sea, purple heathered hills and boldly stark landscapes. It was a wild beauty thrumming with energy. And she loved that he'd been caring enough to want to keep an eye on his father and make sure he was faring well.

"Would ye ever think of staying here?" His amber eyes locked on hers and her heart missed a beat as it jumped in her chest.

She felt as if she could barely take a breath, the air in the room too thin. "Are ye saying what I think ye are? Are ye asking me to stay, Conall?"

He brushed her cheek with the back of his hand, his eyes taking her in and making her feel as if there was no one in the world but the two of them. "Aye, love. I think I am. I know we've not been together long, but I can't stand the thought that ye'll be walking away from what we have a few months from now."

Her brother slid into the seat across from them before she had a chance to respond—which may have been a good thing since she didn't think she could string together a coherent thought the way her mind was racing. This was a huge step.

"At least I didn't get myself barred." Liam shook his head and picked up the menu. "I'm starving."

"I swear, ye have a one-track mind, Liam—and ye're one lucky bastard." Somehow, her brother always managed to get himself out of a pile of shite smelling like a bed of roses. "Ye just better not screw up again. We're here for months, if not longer, and I'll not have ye making our lives here uncomfortable. I like Lara, aye?"

"I like her too, love." Liam's crooked smile made her want to yank his ear like an errant child. "I like her a lot."

"Hmph." She pursed her lips together. "I bet ye do."

Maggie snuck away from Conall's side with a final lingering look at him as he slept, his long limbs and muscular form making her want to crawl back into the comfort of his arms. By the gods, she'd fallen for him fast and hard, and truth was, she couldn't remember ever being happier.

After taking Piper out and settling her down with her favorite chew toy, Maggie got started on breakfast. Going through the cabinets in Conall's modern and sleek kitchen, she was pleased to find that, despite his proclamation of not cooking, his pantry was well stocked. She grabbed the cold butter and flour, and then found the sugar, vanilla extract, almonds, and apricots. Just needed some baking soda, eggs, and milk.

With the oven preheating, she quickly mixed the ingredients together and put the apricot-almond scones in to cook. As the coffee brewed and the scones baked, the kitchen filled with the scents that reminded her of home. It was her mother's recipe, though she'd made them often enough to know the steps by heart.

A knock at the door caught her by surprise. Liam—it was as if he could smell the scones baking. She stepped to the side and let him in.

"Ye're just in time. I've got yer favorite and there's a fresh pot of coffee on." And then she saw the crease in his brow and worried eyes. "What is it? What's wrong?"

"We can't talk here. Meet me back at the bus—and not a word to lover boy, aye?" Liam had already turned and was heading for his car.

Closing the door behind her, she stepped out into the blustery cold and tried to catch up to him. "*Oi!* Hold up, would ye? What's going on?"

Liam spun around to face her, his brown hair catching in the wind. He looked towards the house, paused and then shook his head, leveling his blue eyes on her. "It's Aidan. Flaherty's got him."

Maggie's stomach sunk and then flipped, the blood draining from her face as she grabbed his arm. "What do ye mean Flaherty's got him?"

"They grabbed him last night at gunpoint when he was coming out of the pub and then called Da. They want the Highlander's Hope. They're keeping him until we hand over the jewels." His shoulders sagged as he shook his head, his gaze on the ground. "Ma and Da are beside themselves with worry."

It was like a punch to the gut, her panic rising up to swallow her whole. "But we don't have the jewels and we're still months away from the transfer." She thought of the little blips in security. The alarm going off. Had they been trying to hack her system to try to gain access to the jewels? And after they failed to get through, moved on to a new plan?

"Maggie…we've no choice but to steal them. They know we're working on the security for the jewels and can manage something, even if it takes a while. There's no other option—they'll kill him, yeah? And no one can know—especially if this is going to be a drawn-out affair. Not even Conall." His jaw tightened. "I'm sorry, love, but we can't risk him standing in our way or calling the authorities. Ye'll need to break all ties."

"I can't, Liam. I love him." It was yet another blow. Conall wouldn't risk the Hope—or his reputation. Even worse, he might think the reason for their relationship was nothing more than a front to gain access to his security systems. Yet she wasn't willing to give him up. "I won't tell him anything, but I'm not ending it. He means too much me."

"Ye barely know him, Maggie. And if ye both love each other, then you can make it work once we have Aidan back."

"It's not your decision. I'll deal with it—with Conall." What choice did she have? Leaving Conall wasn't an option—it couldn't be.

Liam shook his head, his lips pressed in a thin line. "I hope ye know what ye're doing then. Because it's Aidan's life that's on the line, yeah? Think about that. 'Cause ye know what the Flahertys are like—they'll be chopping off Aidan's fingers and mailing them to us if they don't think we're taking them seriously."

His words left her fighting back tears, her body shaking uncontrollably as she choked on a sob. Liam pulled her into his arms and held her tightly.

"We'll get him back, love. I just hope that keeping yer man around doesn't turn into a mistake we'll all regret."

CHAPTER
Twelve

THE FRAGRANT SCENT of coffee and baked goods teased Conall awake, like a siren-song pulling him from his slumber. Sleep still clung to the edges of his mind as he rolled over to find his bed empty and Maggie gone. Coffee…and Maggie—the two things he was desperate for. He climbed out of bed and threw on his sweats before padding down the stairs and into an empty kitchen, Piper the only one there.

Noticing the oven was on, he peeked in and found scones browning to a perfect golden brown. Just as he debated whether or not to pull them out, Maggie walked in through the back door. The smile that immediately sprung to his lips upon seeing her quickly faded as he noticed the worry in her eyes, the blue of them shaded to a stormy grey. "What's wrong, love?"

He closed the distance between them just as a small smile made it to her lips and she waved his worries away. "It's nothing—the wind always makes my eyes water."

She gave him a quick kiss and then pulled the scones out of the oven while he watched her, searching for any sign that something was wrong. Needing to feel her close, he sidled up behind her and wrapped his arms around her waist. "So, are these one of yer specialties? Ye spoil me, love."

"It's me ma's recipe." She leaned against him, and pulled his arms even tighter around her, her voice sounding strained.

He leaned forward, still holding her, and kissed her cheek. "Are ye sure ye're all right?"

She looked up at him, her smile tight. "It's nothing. Why don't ye get us a cup of coffee and I'll plate the scones."

Pulling out a couple of mugs from the cabinet, he did as she asked though he couldn't help but glance her way in an attempt to figure out what was bothering her. Because something was certainly wrong, even if she wouldn't admit it.

He handed her a cup of coffee and took the scone she offered him, not another word spoken between them. They sat down at the table, and he took a bite of the hot scone, the taste of it making him fall in love with her all over again. "Damn, woman. These are good."

That earned him a smile—and a genuine one at that. "I'm glad ye like it. Because if you didn't, I might have to take ye out back and beat ye with a thistle."

"Why is it ye always make me want to misbehave?" He teasingly flicked his eyebrows up and ran a hand down her arm, happy to see she was looking more herself. "It's a pity we've got to get to work, since I could easily find ways to waste the day away with you in my arms."

Her smile faded once more, his worries returning. "I love ye, Conall. No matter what ye may think, or what I might do or say, I need ye to know that I love ye."

Her words left him shaken and confused. "Maggie…what's going on?"

"It's nothing." She managed a smile, even as her eyes shimmered with unshed tears. "I'm just having a bit of a rough morning. It'll pass, yeah? Or maybe I should go. I'll need to get ready and head over to the jobsite anyway."

"Maggie...stay. It's still early." Conall wasn't sure what was going on, but if she was upset, he didn't want her shutting him out or pushing him away. "I don't want ye leaving if ye're having a rough time of it. I'm here for ye, aye? If we're in a relationship, it's through thick and thin. Ye can talk to me about anything at all, love. *Anything.*"

This time, her smile—even if it was just a hint of one—reached her eyes. "You're a good man, Conall."

"It's only because you make me want to be a better man." When he brushed her cheek, she leaned into his hand, her eyes locked on his. He kissed her slowly, and then again, nuzzling her with their heads bent together.

When she finally pulled away, whatever had been bothering her seemed to have faded away, her full smile returning, even if he had his doubts that all was well. "Ye best finish up with that breakfast, boyo. I've got plans for you and they involve keeping up yer energy."

He couldn't help but laugh as he pushed his worries away. "As ye wish, love. Wouldn't want to disappoint."

Maggie had left him thoroughly exhausted and satiated, with a kiss and a promise to return once she'd finished working for the day. Conall had plenty to do, but would be working from home—if he could actually concentrate on what he needed to get done. Hours had passed since she'd gone, and he'd yet to get much accomplished, distracted by why Maggie was upset that morning.

Something was up, even if she wouldn't admit to it. Things had been fine between them last night, and she wasn't exactly the sort to overreact with high emotions or drama. But what happened and when? It didn't help that her words continued to haunt him. *"No matter what ye may think, or what I might do or say, I need ye to know that I love ye."* It was as if this was just the start of something, and there were worse things still to come.

He ran a rough hand through his hair and then got to his feet, resisting the urge to pace. It had been far too long since he had to deal with such worries. A part of him wanted to brush it off as paranoia after being single for years but he'd be a fool to ignore the matter completely. He'd have to just let it go for now and see how things progressed, and with luck, it'd be nothing.

He'd get back to work, but first he needed to clear his head. He grabbed his keys and Piper, knowing she'd enjoy the ride, and headed out for a drive along the coast. Wind and rain came in off the sea and lashed at the glass, the sky an angry grey, his windshield wipers thumping offbeat to the music on the radio. Though the weather wasn't cooperating, the drive helped lull his racing mind and his crazy mutt was so happy, he couldn't help but find himself in a better mood.

Not far from town, he decided he'd pay Rowan a visit. Since her gallery and art studio was the only one in the area, the pretty little shop was doing quite well. Of course, Rowan had tried getting him to take an art class or two, but he'd politely declined, his talents lying elsewhere.

Knowing she wouldn't mind Piper tagging along, he parked, clicked the leash into place and then headed to Rowan's gallery. The dainty chimes dangling from the storefront door clinked to announce his arrival as he stepped into the warmth and shelter of the shop.

"Now this is a pleasant surprise." Giving him a wide smile, Rowan bent over and gave his ecstatic pup a scratch, only to pull away cringing. "Ugh…wet dog."

"Had to get out of the house for a bit." He sighed, realizing too late that Rowan was awfully good at reading every little nuance. Already she had one eyebrow perked and her head tilted to the side, her gaze taking in every aspect of him as if she were a hunting dog that had picked up on a scent. "Don't."

"Don't what?" She shrugged, a look of pure innocence on her face.

"Ye want to meddle. Ye just can't help yerself, can ye?" He shook his head as he pursed his lips to keep at bay the smile tugging at his lips.

"If you didn't want me meddling, then you wouldn't have come here." A know-it-all smile danced on her lips. "Well? What's bugging you?"

He sighed again, knowing it might do him some good to talk to her. "I don't know. I guess I'm just not used to being in a relationship. I never know if I'm reading more into something than there actually is."

"You're a smart man, Conall." She leaned up against one of her counters. "I'm not saying there's anything wrong, but if you think something's up, then I'd be inclined to think it might be the case."

He didn't want to go into any detail with Rowan, but Maggie didn't seem the type to come to tears easily, nor did he believe it had been the wind as she had claimed. Had she met up with someone outside? If her brother was staying at Rowan's cottage, he wouldn't be far.

Had Liam given her a hard time about their relationship—about her spending the night at his place? Conall knew firsthand what it was like, since he was none too happy when his sister started dating and things got serious with the lads she was seeing. He could see Maggie and Liam arguing about it, but wasn't so sure it'd lead to tears.

In the end, all he could do is be there for her. "It's nothing. I'm sure it'll get sorted before long, if it's even still an issue."

"Why don't the two of you come by for dinner someday soon? We're heading into the weekend and I could do with some company." Rowan tucked a stray curl behind her ear. "And maybe Maggie's just feeling cooped up since we're so far from the city. I'd imagine it could get to a person if they're not used to being in a place so remote."

"Aye, it could be that I suppose." Or not. He should go see her and get this sorted rather than letting it distract him all day.

His cell phone buzzed in his pocket and then chimed the sound he always dreaded hearing. He glanced at his phone, and swiped through several screens of the report his system had transmitted. "Shite. I've gotta go."

Rowan called after him as he hustled out of her shop, dragging Piper behind him. "Ask her about dinner. Don't forget."

Conall sped his way back home along the winding seaside roads. Something or someone had tried to break through one of the firewalls he'd setup on Iain's systems—the ones he'd designed for the Hope. Coupled with the earlier disturbances Maggie had experienced with her own systems, it left him on edge. He dialed Maggie's cell but it went through to voicemail after several rings.

He pulled down his drive and grabbed Piper, who must have sensed something was wrong and was actually looking subdued. Letting them in, he immediately headed for his computers, and started pulling up screenshots and running diagnostics while trying Maggie again.

This time she picked up. "Maggie—check yer firewalls. My systems detected a disturbance similar to the one ye found with yer systems a few weeks back."

"I'm sorry, love. That was me." Maggie cursed under her breath and then continued, her words coming out in a hurry. "I was messing around with the parameters and making some adjustments. I must have bumped against yer walls and triggered them. I hope I didn't cause ye any problems or worries."

Conall sat back on the sofa with a long sigh of relief. "Nae, love. Dinnae fash yerself. I'm just glad it wasn't anything more."

"Listen…it's been a long day. I think I'm going to spend the night at the cottage, if that's all right with you."

"I can't say ye won't be missed." A wave of worry roiled in his gut, impossible to ignore. He hated having these sorts of conversations over the phone. It left him completely blind to the clues a person's facial expressions would normally provide. Instead, he was left trying to decipher the inflections in her tone and voice. "Maggie…if there's something wrong… I'm here for ye, love."

"I know ye are—and I truly appreciate it."

CHAPTER
Thirteen

GUILT OVERWHELMED MAGGIE as she hung up the phone with Conall. She was desperate to see him, to tell him everything. Yet she couldn't tell Conall. He'd never let her steal the Hope—not even for her brother—and he'd feel compelled to tell Iain, who would likely get the authorities involved.

Worse still, she'd have to explain her family's connection to the Flahertys. It was because of her father's past and his acquaintances that the jewels and her brother were now in jeopardy. And she could only imagine Conall's reaction if he ever found out that her father had been a thief of some renown, given that he, too, was in the security business and it could ruin his reputation if it got out. It was something she should have told him when they were discussing their pasts and promised to be completely honest with each other. Yet she hadn't.

Conall had wanted complete and total honesty between them, and instead she was honoring that request with avoidance and deceptions.

It had been harder than she thought to spend time with him when she couldn't be completely honest with all that was happening. She felt like she was under a magnifying glass, for the man missed nothing, and if she continued to spend time with him, he'd know something was drastically wrong. Keeping her distance was the only way she'd manage to keep her lies to a minimum. It was the least she could do, and maybe, when it was all over and Aidan was home safe, Conall might forgive her.

"Ye've got a puss on ye, Maggie." Liam could never resist teasing her, even if he should know better by now—especially given the circumstances.

"I'm warning ye, I'm in no mood." She glared at him, but his smile only widened. "I'm glad ye're able to find the humor in our brother getting kidnapped and my life going to hell."

His smile quickly faded. "Do ye not think I'm worried? Well, I am— and you know it. But what option do we have? If ye've got some grand plan, by all means, I'm listening—'cause I've got nothing."

She pushed past him, needing to get away from the confines of the cramped bus and into the fresh air, grabbing her leather jacket as she took the steps. Digging the keys out of the front pocket of her jeans, she pulled on her helmet, kick-started her bike and tore out onto the road, spraying dirt and gravel. She didn't know where the hell she was going, but hoped the low rumble of the engine and the open road would help clear her head.

She kept going until she lost track of time, and the sun started to set. Under normal circumstances, she'd be heading to Conall's. Except that she wasn't. She couldn't. Not if she wanted to keep her lies to a minimum and her brother safe.

Eventually, she decided to turn back. Desperate to thaw out from the cold wind that whipped in off the sea, she headed into town for a sorely-needed pint. Walking into the pub, she had to beat back the hope that Conall was there, tucked away in a corner having his dinner. She needed to keep her distance, and yet every cell in her body yearned to go to him. Yearned to have him by her side. Yearned for the comfort of his touch.

"A pint of the black, if ye'd be so kind, Lara." Maggie slipped onto the stool and propped her head in her hand, elbow to the bar.

Lara started to pour her a Guinness as Maggie watched the brew dance and swirl within the glass, black and tan, the creamy thick head rising to the top. "Rough day?"

Maggie shrugged and slid Lara some money. "Yeah, I guess."

Lara gave her a kind smile. "Well, I know something that might turn yer day around—a friend of yers is here. And he's a tall drink of water on a hot summer day."

She sat up with a bit of a smile, her gaze scanning the crowds. "Conall's here?"

"Don't be daft. If I was going to say anything about Conall Stewart, it'd be that he was a cantankerous pain in the arse—though you've certainly put him in a better mood as of late." Lara tilted her head towards one of the high backed booths. "This lad's from Dublin."

It couldn't be her brother, Patrick. He'd have called with all that was happening. However…Maggie felt the blood in her face drain, leaving her skin cold and numb, while her heart beat a deafening staccato in her head. "Did he give his name?"

Lara frowned at her, brows drawn together as she took Maggie in. "Are ye all right?"

"*His name, Lara.* Did he give his name?"

"Aye—said it was Sean. Here he is now." Lara flicked her chin towards the booths she'd gestured to just moments earlier, though Maggie barely registered any of it.

Rage and hatred mixed into a volatile combination, and the only thing containing it was the fear for her brother's life. Maggie spun to face him, her eyes locked on his, her body vibrating with the tension it took to keep from murdering the bastard.

"Maggie, love. There ye are." Sean leaned in and kissed her cheek, before whispering in her ear. "Don't go making a scene now, love. Would hate it if anything happened to that gobshite brother of yours."

She ground her teeth to keep the curses from escaping. "If ye'll excuse us, Lara."

Lara's mouth quirked into a bit of a frown. "Aye, but if ye need me for anything, I'm right here."

Sean steered her towards the booth he'd been sitting in, but she shrugged out of his grasp and took a seat. "What the hell are ye doing here?"

Sean's smirk had her wanting to reach over and punch it off his face. "Someone's gotta keep an eye on ye, sweet Maggie. This is our only chance, and I'll not have it going awry. I know what ye're like, yeah?"

"You may think ye know me, but it couldn't be further from the truth." She got to her feet, ready to go. "So let me make myself clear. Harm a hair on Aidan's head, and I'll kill ye myself."

"I did always like that feistiness. But be careful, yeah? Wouldn't want ye getting yerself or yer brother into trouble. And be thankful I didn't make you part of the deal. I could have—and still might." The corner of his mouth kicked up into a menacing sneer. "Don't ye remember how fun it was? Except ye thought yerself better than the rest of us. Yer whole family did—the high and almighty Brennans."

She scoffed at him, fire in her eyes. "High and almighty, indeed. But truth is, anyone would have to fall pretty damn far to stoop down to yer level."

"Yeah. I'll do my best to avoid him, Da. Don't go worrying. Just take care of yourselves over there. I'll let ye know if anything changes. And I swear, Da, we'll get Aidan back." Maggie finished her goodbyes and hung up the phone.

"So, what did Sean say?" Liam was watching her, arms crossed in front of his chest as he leaned against the counter in the cottage, but she was in no mood to discuss Sean or what they were going to do about Aidan.

"I'll deal with him—with this." Her mind was racing through the details as a plan started to form.

It'd be a huge risk, but truth was she didn't know if she'd be able to get her hands on the Hope anytime soon. They were still months away from completing the security systems and that meant the jewels were hidden away someplace safe. She didn't even know where, let alone know how to steal them.

If, however, she managed to create a tracking device small and inconspicuous enough to hide on the necklace itself…then maybe she could use it as an excuse to gain access to the jewels. And if she did manage to steal it, this would at least aid in its safe return.

It had to work. Had to. 'Cause she had nothing else. She'd get her brother back, even if it ruined everything she'd worked so hard for.

There was something else bothering her, though. Clearly, it was no coincidence that she'd run into Sean just now in Dunmuir. But Dublin? At first she'd thought it nothing but rotten luck that they'd seen him while wandering the city. But now? She had to wonder if it was the start of Sean's plan. Had he been following her, knowing they'd soon snag her brother? Yet the trip to Dublin had been a spur of the moment thing.

The chance of it being sheer coincidence seemed slim. And that meant that Sean somehow knew she was going to Dublin or they'd been keeping tabs on her da's home. It'd likely be the latter, but it made her wonder if things were as secure as she'd hoped here in Dunmuir. The bus and Conall's home would be hard to tap or break into, but the cottage was a different story. Had she discussed going to Dublin while at the cottage? The bus? The museum grounds? She couldn't really remember the details, but it made her leery and suspicious. Like someone had been watching and listening all along.

Her brother pulled her from her thoughts. "Maggie…ye don't need to do this alone, love. Tell me what I can do to help."

She reached out and squeezed his hand to keep him from worrying. It wasn't that she didn't want to tell him, but if the cabin was bugged, then she didn't want to risk saying anything. "I could do with some fresh air. Ye mind joining me?"

He nodded, his brows drawn together in worry. "Aye, love. Anything ye want."

They stepped out into the cold as the wind coming in off the sea whipped around them and the light from the cottage struggled against the inky darkness. She wrapped her arms around herself to try to ward off the bone-numbing chill, and then told her brother of her suspicions.

"The bastards. I wonder how long they've been planning this." He shook his head, the coiled tension pouring off of him as he cursed under his breath. "They must think us gombeens."

"Until we know how they're keeping tabs on us, we'll have to watch what we say and who we say it to. And we'll need to sweep for bugs— everywhere. The bus, the cottage, the museum. Conall's place is likely secure, but it might be a good idea to check there also if I can figure out a way to check without him growing suspicious." At least she'd have an excuse to see him again.

It was a small plus in what felt like a whole lot of minuses. She told herself she should be staying away, yet she couldn't bear it. It'd been just over twelve hours since she'd last seen him, and it was already killing her, her feelings no doubt amplified by the thought that there'd be no relief to this nightmare anytime soon. She couldn't possibly stay away until this was resolved, and yet she'd have to try to do just that.

Liam stuffed his hands in his pockets. "How are ye holding up, love?"

She let out a weary and ragged breath, as if his question gave her permission to let down her guard and acknowledge how she felt. "I'm worried, Liam. About so much—about Aidan, the Flahertys, the jewels…"

"And Conall?"

"Yeah. And Conall." She had to blink back the tears that threatened, grateful for the cover of darkness and that she could easily blame it on the wind. "It's been a long time since I last cared about anyone like this, and now..."

Her brother pulled her into a one-armed hug. "I know, darling. I remember what ye went through. You've got a lot to lose."

"I want to tell him, Liam. He might be able to help." She had to believe Conall would understand the position she was in. He wouldn't risk her brother's life for the jewels and his reputation—or would he? She was just so desperate to see him, to smooth things between them. Keeping the truth from him had her gut in knots and uncertainty had her head spinning.

"Maggie, ye can't. If he tells the authorities, it could cost us Aidan's life." He gently placed both hands on her shoulder. "Promise me you won't say anything."

She swiped at the tears that finally escaped, knowing that if she continued to push Conall away and lie to him, she'd lose him forever, their trust shattered. It was the one thing he'd asked for and she'd agreed to. Yet it was mere days later, and she'd already gone against her word.

"Promise me, Maggie." Liam all but shook her in his panic. "We can't risk it."

"I promise." Even if it cost her her heart.

Every time Maggie reached out for Conall, she found herself alone in an empty bed. She spent the night tossing and turning, sleep escaping her as she longed to have him near, his comforting arms wrapped around her.

By the time she crawled out of bed, it felt like she'd been hit by a truck. Even worse, her heart ached like it'd been wrenched from her body, leaving her an empty and broken shell. Lying to Conall and keeping him at bay was eating her up. It left her feeling hollow and incomplete. Add to that constantly worrying about her brother and the danger he was in, and she was a bundle of nerves.

Showering helped her wake up, but her mind kept churning over what she should do about Aidan and Conall. She stumbled into the kitchen and got a pot of coffee going, ignoring Liam, who was shoveling in a big fry up of eggs, rashers, bangers, tomato, and a stack of generously buttered toast.

"There's a pot of tea made." He looked at her over his pile of salty meat. "Ye look like shite, Maggie. Didn't sleep well?"

"What do you think?" She glared at her brother, thinking it was going to be one cursedly long day if he was going to constantly point out the obvious. "And if anyone doesn't care for my appearance, then they can look elsewhere. I'm not the fecking Rose of Tralee, Liam."

He threw his hands up in mock surrender. "Didn't say ye were, love."

She gave him a final scowl, ignoring that his words could be taken as yet another jab, and stole one of his greasy bangers, taking a bite. "We need to do a sweep of the bus and see if we can manage the museum." They'd already cleared the cottage and found nothing.

Finishing up his breakfast in record time, Liam dropped his dish in the sink, ran some hot water over it, and drank the last of his tea. "I'm heading in."

He'd yet to move when there was a knock at the door. "Stay here in case it's Sean. I'd rather not have to explain to Seamus Flaherty why his son has a knife sticking out of him—especially since in the mood ye're in, I'd say it's a distinct possibility I'd end up having to do just that."

She certainly wasn't going to argue with him when there was a good chance he was right. But it wasn't Sean—it was Conall—and Liam was trying to send him away. She headed for the front door, only to find Liam standing there with his hands on the doorjamb, blocking the entry so Conall couldn't pass or see past him. "Sorry, she's busy. I'll tell her you stopped by, though."

"I've got it, Liam." Maggie came up behind her brother and waited for him to get out of the way. Not that he was going anywhere. "If ye don't mind, I'd appreciate a bit of privacy."

"I'm heading to work. Don't be too long, yeah?" Liam grabbed his jacket and pushed past them, his brow furrowed as he shook his head and headed for the truck.

Maggie stepped to the side, holding onto her arms, suddenly feeling chilled, her bad mood turning sullen. All she wanted was for things to go back to normal. For her brother to be home safe. For her to not have to push Conall away. "Sorry about that."

Conall threw her a worried glance before moving past her and into the room. She resisted the urge to touch him, to wrap her arms around him and tell him everything. All she wanted was for him to hold her and tell her it would be all right, unable to put any distance between them.

As if knowing exactly what she needed, he pulled her into his arms and touched her cheek, his eyes searching hers. Her breath caught when his thumb brushed her lips and then, as if nothing else mattered, as if all would be well if they had each other, he kissed her. Kissed her until all else melted away, and it was just the two of them. Kissed her as if he alone could sustain her, as if he were her very breath and the blood in her veins, as if he were her beating heart.

His kisses eventually slowed, but she couldn't pull away. Instead, they stood there with their heads bowed together, their lips just a whisper away, his arms pulling her into his embrace.

When he spoke, his voice was thick with emotion and need. "I missed ye, Maggie."

"I missed you, too." She threw her arms around his neck and held tightly, wishing the rest of the world and all its problems would just disappear.

She buried her head in the crook of his neck, breathing in his familiar scent and taking comfort in his arms. He stroked her hair and cradled her, holding her close, but his ragged breath had her beating back tears, knowing she'd soon have to push him away again.

He pulled away just enough to hold her face in his hands, his gaze drifting over her features as if trying to find an answer to what was wrong. "Och, love…what's happening? And don't tell me it's nothing. I've never seen so drastic a change in a person. Don't shut me out, Maggie. I'm begging ye to not push me away."

Yet what choice did she have?

CHAPTER Fourteen

WHEN MAGGIE COULDN'T look him in the eyes, he suddenly realized just how bad things had gotten between them—and in such a short amount of time. "Maggie, please. Talk to me, damn it. What the hell's going on?"

The last thing he wanted was to get angry with her, but he couldn't deal with not knowing what was wrong. It didn't help that sleeping without her tucked in at his side left him tossing and turning and in one hell of a bad mood come morning.

"I love ye, Conall. But right now, I need that to be enough for you. Just know that ye're my very heart." She cupped his cheek and nuzzled him close, kissed him with a brush of her lips, slow and sweet.

Was he blowing the matter out of proportion? Damn it. *This* was why he didn't get involved in relationships. Not that she wasn't worth it. He couldn't remember being happier—until yesterday.

"Is this because of yer brother? Is Liam giving ye a hard time?" If that was it, he'd make amends, even if they'd done nothing wrong. "I know I got off to a rocky start with him, but bloody hell, Maggie. Ye can't let him get between us, love—not for something that's none of his business."

She shook her head no with a sigh. "It's not that. And trust me when I tell ye, I don't want anything coming between us."

"Then what's changed, love? Ye were so happy, so full of life, just days ago. And now…ye're a shadow of who ye were. I love ye and I want to help, but I can't if ye won't let me in. And damn it, Maggie, I don't want to lose ye." Didn't she see what this was doing to him? How could everything deteriorate so quickly? She'd said she'd battled with depression before. Was that the problem? A bad breakup had brought it on before. But now? Everything had been perfect. They'd been happy.

She led him to the sofa, shifting in her seat so she could face him. When she bit her bottom lip and ran her hands down her jeans, he took her hand in his to try to comfort her.

"I know I've been distant." She managed a smile, even if it didn't reach her eyes. "I've got some other stuff going on and have been under a lot of stress. I shouldn't have let it get to me—or let it affect our relationship—and for that, I'm really sorry."

He wanted to press her for answers, to remind her that they'd both agreed to be honest. Yet she hadn't lied to him, but rather refused to tell him what the hell was going on. He let out a weary breath. Pulling her to him, he kissed her head, happy he could still hold her in his arms. He'd try to give her more time, more space.

Brushing a stray curl from her eyes, his touch lingered. He needed to have her close, needed the connection between them to keep his uncertainties at bay. "It's the industry we're in, love. Things can get complicated. But if there's anything I can do to help, all ye need to do is ask. I'm pretty good at what I do, if I might say so myself."

Her lips quirked into a hint of a smile—a real one—even if it was overshadowed by whatever was upsetting her. "There'd be no denying that, love."

"And I've got good instincts, Maggie. Ye have to in this line of work." Which is why this felt bigger than work.

"I don't want to talk about this anymore—and I want things to get back to normal between us. I don't know how things got so strained between us and in so little time." Shifting closer to him, she ran a hand down his arm and bit her bottom lip. "And since it's my fault, let me make it up to ye."

When she straddled his lap and kissed him, he pulled her close, running his hands down her back until they rested at the luscious curve of her waist. A small part of his brain told him this was nothing more than a distraction technique. A way to change the subject. Yet it didn't matter in that moment—not when she was in his arms.

Her kiss deepened, but Conall's doubts and thoughts continued to nag at him. Things felt so different between them. Her passion felt…not quite forced, but…distracted. Like she was going through the motions, her heart not in it. He slowed their kisses and pulled away, cupping her face in his hands and searching her eyes for answers.

"Och, love…Let me in. Ye can't tell me this is a simple work issue. Not when everything about ye feels off. I'm here for ye, love. Ye know that, aye? Ye can trust me, Maggie. Let me help."

She pulled away and shook her head, climbing off his lap to pace. "I do trust ye."

"But?" He waited for her to say something. Anything. But when she refused to speak to him, he tried unsuccessfully to beat back his frustration. He leaned back on the sofa and ran his hand down his face.

Her eyes locked on his, his own frustration mirrored in her eyes. "What do ye want me to say, Conall? If I could include ye in this goddamned mess, then don't ye think I would? But I can't, damn it. Our relationship isn't the only thing on the line here. I'm asking for a bit of space and consideration where this is issue is concerned. And if ye can't give me that, then maybe you should go." Those last words were spoken through a trembling jaw, her eyes shimmering with tears that refused to fall.

"I'll go if ye want me to, but bloody hell, Maggie, I'm only trying to help." Conall got to his feet and started heading for the door, wondering how it could all go so cursedly wrong.

For a moment, she looked like she might actually stop him from going, stop him from walking away.

But she didn't.

By the end of the day, Conall was desperate for a distraction. Anything to keep himself from replaying Maggie's every word, over and over again. He couldn't see how or why everything had fallen to pieces. Had he asked for too much, or taken things too fast? Probably, though she'd seemed happy enough—until it all went to hell.

Was it any wonder he avoided relationships? He liked things to make sense, liked things to remain even-keeled. And relationships were *never* that.

"Maybe you're just reading too much into it." Rowan sat in the booth across from Conall with Angus at her side. She'd checked in on him, and then stated that a pint and a bit of company would be just the thing to cheer him up—whether he was in the mood to go the pub or not. "The impression I got is that she really likes you. And you just got back from Dublin. You said it went well, right?"

"Yes. No." Conall sighed and played with his pint glass, picking it up and putting it down to leave interlocking rings of moisture on the surface of the well-polished table. "I don't know. Parts of it were…amazing. But there were also awkward moments, like meeting her family—who were none too happy about her dating anyone at all, let alone someone who'd likely drag their daughter off to the middle of nowhere. We also ran into her ex. Always a fun experience."

Angus sat back and laughed. "Isn't that always the worst? Rowan's ex still sends her roses. Regularly."

"At least he's on another continent—unlike *your* exes." Rowan bumped Angus with her shoulder, throwing him a teasing smile. "It only took Lara two months and someone trying to kill me before she'd stop glaring at me."

"I don't know…Things were fine once we got back. I couldn't have been happier—and she was happy too. I swear it." He let out a deep breath, his chest tight with worry. "Then yesterday, everything changed. She'd spent the night and by the time I woke up come morning, things felt off between us, felt wrong. And now? She's barely talking to me, damn it."

It took all the energy he had to not punch the wall. Frustration knotted his muscles, his chest tight, every breath an effort. This was the exact reason he avoided anything more than a one-night stand. And yet…He let out a weary sigh. He'd happily walk over hot coals if she was waiting for him at the end of it.

Problem was, she wasn't. She wasn't there.

Rowan reached out and squeezed his hand. "Are you sure there's actually a problem? Maybe she's just in a bit of a mood. It's not like you're all peaches and cream every moment of every day."

He raised his brows at that one. "She's like night and day, Rowan. I wish it was just a bit of a mood that would soon pass, but…" His mind wandered to the depression she'd struggled with, but…this felt different.

"Then maybe it's something she needs to work out on her own. I'm sure, once that's sorted, everything will be back to normal. I've seen the way she looks at you, Conall. Don't give up on her just yet."

"Believe me when I tell ye, that's the last thing I want to do." He loved her, damn it. And she loved him. So what the hell was the bloody problem?

A commotion at the bar pulled him from his thoughts. Lara was none too happy with one of her customers, the bloke getting more than an earful as she attempted to chuck him out. Not that the guy was moving fast enough for her taste, as her curses rode high above the noise in the pub.

As the man turned towards Lara, Conall saw his face—and it was as if the earth was falling out from under him. Sean. Maggie's ex.

Suddenly, everything he thought, everything he believed, was pulled into question.

Barely realizing he was in motion, he caught Sean as he headed for the door. "What the hell are ye doing in Dunmuir?"

Sean looked at him as if trying to place him, before recognition settled on his features, all of it an act. "Ah. Maggie's friend, yeah?"

Conall's hands curled into fists, his anger fueled by suspicion and his past hurts. There was only one logical reason why Sean was in Dunmuir and that was Maggie. "More than her friend."

Sean scoffed. "Is that what she led ye to believe? Ye poor sod. And you were daft enough to believe her? Didn't ye know, there's nothing Maggie likes more than to play those sorts of games."

Anger boiled in Conall's chest, but Angus had hold of his arm and pulled him away before things escalated. "Leave it, aye? He's not worth it."

With a grin, Sean stepped forward. "I'll be sure to tell her you send yer regards."

Conall struggled against Angus but couldn't get free of his friend's grip. "He's just goading ye, aye? It means nothing."

Once Sean was gone, Angus loosened his hold but didn't let go completely, as if testing to see if Conall would go after the bastard. Conall took a deep breath to steady himself and get control of his anger.

"I can't believe that arse." Lara looked ready to murder Sean if he showed his face again. It was clear Conall had at least one formidable ally. "Tell Maggie that I'm sorry. She's always welcome here, but that friend of hers is barred. The cheek of him!"

"Her friend? Is that what he said?" Conall ran a rough hand down his face and tried to push his anger to the side.

She pulled another pint, her gaze still on the door. "Aye—when she was here with him the other night. Though what she's doing with that arse, I haven't a clue."

The other night…The only night they'd been apart was last night—when she'd cancelled their plans together. "When, Lara? When was she here—with Sean?"

"Last night. Sat in the booth right next to the one ye're in."

He turned to Angus, barely able to get the words out through his clenched jaw. "I have to go."

Angus grabbed his arm. "Are ye going to tell me what the hell's going on?"

"I need to talk to Maggie. If ye'll excuse me."

As he drove to Maggie's cottage, his thoughts and doubts, the hurt and betrayal, were all-consuming. Yet he wasn't ready to give up on her, still hoping there was a logical explanation.

Part of him wanted to think that she and Sean were nothing more than friends—or that Sean had shown up on his own. But then why not just tell him? Why push him away?

His anger flared again as Sean's words haunted him. If she had gotten back together with her ex, if she had cheated on him, if she thought this nothing more than a game, it was a betrayal he didn't think he'd recover from.

It was bad enough to go through it with Janet, but Maggie…He'd been so sure she was different. So sure of what they had. Of them. He thought he'd found the one. So how could he be so mistaken?

He pulled down Maggie's drive, relieved to see that there weren't any unfamiliar vehicles. This would be a difficult enough conversation to have without having Sean there to taunt him. And a good thing, too, since he might have to murder the bastard.

Of course it was Liam who answered the door. "I need to see Maggie."

"She's busy." Liam got ready to close the door when Conall stopped him with a firm hand on the door's surface. "Look…I like ye, but ye need to go—and ye need to leave my sister alone."

"The only way that's going to happen is if I talk to her first. If ye want me gone, the fastest way to accomplish that is to let me see her." By the gods, he'd fight his way to her if he had to. He needed answers. He needed to know the truth. Because, more than anything, it would be the uncertainty that would kill him.

"Ye're better off forgetting about her. Move on, yeah?" Liam stood up straight, his gaze challenging. "As for work, ye'll now be dealing with me if ye need anything."

"I'm not going, Liam. Not until I see her one last time." Conall debated his options, but there were few outside of sheer stubbornness. And then he spotted Maggie at the top of the stairs. "*Maggie!*"

She wrapped her arms around herself, as if warding off a chill, but she didn't come any closer.

"I'm not leaving until ye talk to me." Though he was desperate for answers, seeing her again had his emotions in a tumult.

He breathed a little easier when she came down the stairs. "It's fine, Liam."

Liam cursed under his breath, but left with a final glare at Conall and unspoken words between him and his sister. As Maggie approached, Conall couldn't help but notice the dark circles under her red eyes. It left him torn. Part of him wanted to take her in his arms and comfort her, and the other part of him was still furious about Sean.

"I could do with a whisky. You?" Maggie stepped to the side to let him in, and then headed to the cabinet where there was a bottle of Jameson and a couple of glasses sitting on a small tray.

"Aye. May as well." Conall thanked her for the drink and took a long sip, the heat of it like molten glass as it slipped down his throat and warmed him from the inside. It was just the fortification he needed. "I don't mean to bother ye, Maggie, but I need answers and I need the truth."

"Conall…things aren't always that simple. Ye're always looking for things to be black and white, and they're not. They're every shade in between. Nothing is ever so clear cut." She let out a weary sigh and hung her head, as if the mere sight of him was too much to bear.

"I sure as hell didn't think the way we felt about each other was just another grey area, Maggie. Sorry for being so foolish." He grit his teeth to keep from swearing up a storm.

She looked away and bit her bottom lip, wrapping her arms around herself. "What do you want me to say, Conall? Things got a bit intense and I needed a break. Some space."

"I could see that. Things did get intense." Conall took another deep breath. "So, last night…I hope ye managed a quiet night at home. Did it help?"

She glanced at him and then looked away, her gaze avoiding his as she spoke. "Yeah. Time alone helped."

"I don't suppose ye want to try looking at me if ye're going to lie," Conall scoffed, not quite wanting to believe that history was repeating itself. "I know you were with Sean, Maggie. And damn it, if ye didn't want to be with me, then ye could have bloody well said so." With his heart breaking and feeling a fool, he turned to leave.

She grabbed his arm. "Wait. Don't go."

She took a step towards him, but his hurt had him backing away. "Why shouldn't I? Or are ye going to tell me Sean's just one more shade of grey?"

Tears rolled down her cheeks. "I never wanted to hurt ye, Conall. I hope ye know that."

"Aye, well, not lying to me would've been a good start." He took a deep breath to calm himself, and to push away the tumult of emotions that threatened. "It was the only thing I'd asked for. A bit of honesty. At least now I know the truth. I know where we stand."

Her eyes finally locked on his, as if daring him to look away, her gaze fierce. "You know nothing, Conall. Not a single thing."

CHAPTER
Fifteen

O F COURSE, MAGGIE still had to work with Conall, which only served to remind her why she'd fallen for him so hard. He'd done his best to avoid her, but Iain had informed them that they would be housing a few more precious items, and so a change had to be made to the schematics. Not exactly her brother's area of expertise.

She had drafted up the first of the changes she'd be making and now waited for Conall to look them over and make his recommendations. He had his head bent over the papers she'd given him, his dark honey locks scruffy and unkempt, matching the thick stubble across his handsome face. Her heart ached for him, and she longed to have him close, making her want to tell him everything so he could take her in his arms and tell her everything would be fine.

"I'll put yer changes in place once we finalize them." He turned those intense amber eyes on her and then frowned, as he took her in. "Are ye all right?"

Hearing the weariness in his voice had her blinking away the tears that always seemed to threaten as of late. "Yeah. I'm fine."

He took a step towards her, but it seemed he'd done so out of habit, and stopped as if remembering they were no longer together. His jaw tightened and his eyes hardened, making her heart ache all the more. "It was yer decision, Maggie. I'm sorry if it no longer suits ye."

Her decision. She scoffed in disbelief. As if this were exactly how she had wanted her life to unfold. She'd found the perfect man, only to have it ruined by lies she was forced to tell. "I still love ye, Conall."

He shook his head, his breathing heavy as those beautiful gold eyes turned hard. "What the hell am I supposed to do with that, Maggie? Do ye think this is easy for me? Cause I can tell ye that it isn't, damn it."

"Well, it's not like I'm dancing around in my party-knickers either. I've never been more miserable, Conall." She turned away and swiped at her tears, cursing herself for being so weak. But it was all too much, and her emotions had been running high ever since those bastards took Aidan.

"Ye should have thought of that before ye promised me honesty and then lied to me with the same breath." He pounded the work table with a fist, making the pens jump. "Ye made yer bed."

As if the gods must truly have it out for her, Iain and Andrew walked into the workroom. "I've gotta go." Luckily, there was a back door. Ignoring Conall's curses, she bolted for it, not wanting the others to see her crying. She'd catch up with Iain after she'd had a chance to calm herself and dry her eyes.

"*Maggie.* Hold up, would ye?" Conall caught up to her, his long stride closing the distance between them with ease. When she didn't stop, he grabbed her arm and spun her to face him. She was helpless to keep her tears from falling, and though she refused to look at him, it did little to hide the state she was in.

The silence stretched out between them until he let out a weary sigh. "Och, love…I wish ye'd tell me what the hell's gone wrong."

The kindness in his voice, despite everything they'd recently been through, gave her the hope and courage she needed to look at him. "I wish I could tell ye, love, but I can't."

The hard edge to his voice and gaze was back. "Can't or won't? Because I've offered to be there for ye, offered my help and support, and ye've still turned me away, still lied to me."

The words sat there on the tip of her tongue, desperate to escape, to tell him everything. Yet the thought of Aidan coming to harm left her second-guessing everything her heart was telling her she should do. "I said can't. I *can't* tell ye. I was happy, Conall. Happier than I've ever been. So why the hell would I put all that on the line?"

He threw his hands up and shook his head. "Clearly, I haven't a clue, Maggie. And this is going nowhere if ye don't let me in on what's happening with ye. I'm not a bloody mindreader, aye?"

When she said nothing, he let out a weary sigh and hung his head. "I can't do this, love. I can't. Like ye said—life's too short. And it's certainly too short to spend it with someone who doesn't trust me. Sorry we couldn't make it work. I think we would have been happy together."

"I've no doubt we would have."

Maggie turned away and squeezed her eyes shut the moment she realized that the video was of her brother, his captors sending a clear message. They were losing patience and Aidan was running out of time. Fury competed with fear as she swiped at her tears.

Liam paced the floor of their cottage. "I swear I'll murder each and every one of them once we get Aidan back."

"What if we go to the authorities? Surely they'll have more experience with this sort of thing." They had to get Aidan back. And trying to steal the jewels was taking too long. She was still working on the tracking device she'd attach to the necklace, but getting it to look completely inconspicuous was proving difficult. She'd get there—but she needed more time, and it was clear that was the one thing they didn't have a lot of.

"It'd be a huge risk, Maggie." Liam rubbed his forehead as if trying to ward off a headache, weariness in his every move. "I don't know. Sean's in town now and we still haven't figured out how they knew you were heading to Dublin."

"I know ye don't want me saying anything to Conall, but he might be able to help." At least then she could come clean. Lying to him about Sean and seeing how her betrayal hurt him left her feeling like the lowest of scum. How could she do that to him? Especially after all he'd been through.

She'd been hoping that once they had Aidan back and she'd come clean, he'd understand and forgive her. But that was before Sean showed up and had Conall thinking she'd cheated on him. Conall might understand why she didn't tell him what was going on, but she doubted he'd be quick to trust her again. Not when he thought she'd hooked up with Sean, even if that wasn't the case.

And that crushed her.

"How could he possibly help?" He let out a ragged breath that seemed to come from his very core. "Maggie…I know this is hard on ye, but we need to keep our heads. Aidan's life depends on it."

"Which is why I want to include Conall. I've not met a smarter man, and he'd do what he could to help us." Then she'd be able to tell him the truth and try to salvage what they had. The longer she waited, the worse things got between them and the less chance there'd be of him ever forgiving her. And the truth of the matter was, he *could* help get Aidan back.

Liam shook his head in frustration and continued to pace. "Or he could turn us in to Iain MacCraigh and get Aidan killed—not to mention ruin us."

"He wouldn't do that knowing Aidan's life's on the line. He wouldn't turn us in." Not if he still loved her.

"Well, he sure as hell isn't going to let us steal the Hope, either. And if ye think he would, then ye're daft."

"I'm going for a walk." She needed some air. Needed to get away. Needed to think.

He looked at her in disbelief. "Maggie…ye'll get yerself killed. It's dark and the cliffs plunge right into the ocean."

"I'll take my chances." She was already shrugging into her jacket and zipping it shut, knowing the winds could be fierce coming in off the sea. Ignoring Liam's curses, she stepped out into the open air. Lucky for her, the moon was close to full, cutting down on the chances that they'd be fishing her dead body out of the sea.

Out of habit, she wandered towards Conall's home, though she had no real intention of seeing him. It had been days since she'd last spoken to him, their relationship still in pieces. Conall seemed to now prefer working from home so he could avoid her at all cost.

Yet she was desperate to see him. To tell him everything so he could see her betrayal and lies weren't because she was trying to hurt him. If she could just get her brother back home safely. Surely he would see why she couldn't have told him the truth.

But how the hell was she supposed to get the Hope? It was currently being guarded in an undisclosed location, and she was sure the security measures in place would be top rate. But what if…

Instead of trying to get the Hope, could she instead just try to get her brother? They'd likely be holding him somewhere in Ireland, since transporting Aidan out of the country without drawing attention would be difficult. But how could she track him down? Cell phones and signal towers might work. She could also track credit card purchases and bank withdrawals. But could she pull off that sort of hacking? Her expertise was primarily in the building of security equipment. She was good with computers and computer security, but this was something completely different. There was, however, one person near and dear to her heart who was amazing at it.

"A bit late to be going for a walk, don't ye think?"

Maggie spun towards the voice, her heart racing. It sounded familiar, but in the dark, she couldn't make out who it belonged to. So close to Conall's, she'd expect him to be the only one wandering about the heathered fields by the cliff, yet she knew his voice and it wasn't him.

The accent wasn't Scottish either. "Andrew?"

He stepped closer so she could finally make out his face. "Yeah…sorry. Didn't mean to startle you. I was going to stop by the cottage to see if I could interest you in dinner, when I saw you head out."

With no one else around, Andrew's presence had her shoulders going tense. "My brother and I ate already."

"How about a pint then?" He shoved his hands in his pockets and took a small step closer.

She shifted and got ready to run. Maybe she was being paranoid, but better safe than sorry. Her life was a big enough mess without adding to her problems. "I was just heading to Conall's. Those are his lights there in the distance."

"Conall? Really?" Andrew's laugh sent a chill crawling over her skin. "I thought that was over."

"Not at all. We're still together and quite happy, thank ye very much." She was starting to wonder if there was more to Andrew's interest. Most guys weren't so daft when it came to picking up on the clues that someone wasn't interested. It had her growing suspicious.

If she could just put some distance between them. Just in case she was right. Conall's home wasn't far. Maggie started walking. "If ye'll excuse me, I need to go. Conall's expecting me."

"Let me walk you there, at least. It's dark and you could easily twist an ankle." When Andrew joined her, she stopped and turned towards him.

"I'd rather ye don't. I've tried subtlety, but that doesn't seem to be working, so let me make it clear—I'm not interested in yer company, and I'd appreciate ye leaving me alone." She turned and started walking as fast as she could when he grabbed her arm.

"I'm sorry, Maggie. Don't go. There's still so much we need to discuss."

CHAPTER Sixteen

CONALL TWEAKED THE seasoning of the spicy pork he had simmering away, the kitchen windows steamed white with condensation. He ignored Piper, who was doing her best to beg for food—or at the very least be there on the off chance something fell to the floor. Conall didn't know how to cook a huge variety of things, but what he could manage, he did well. Nearly done, he'd pair it with a bit of jasmine rice. It was a simple and hearty meal, the spiciness of it comforting on such a chilly night.

The doorbell rang—and rang again—as Piper threw her head back and let out a high-pitched howl which ended in a chorus of yips. Curious and annoyed, he abandoned his cooking and went to find out who the hell was visiting so late in the evening.

Yanking the door open, his curses died on his lips as his heart plummeted and Maggie stumbled into his arms, ice cold. "What's happened?"

"Lock the door." Maggie looked shaken and scared, but Conall didn't see any injuries.

He pulled her in while searching the darkness just beyond her. There didn't seem to be anyone out there, but he wasn't taking any chances, and locked the door once she was safely inside. Now he just needed to find out what the hell was actually going on.

Motioning her towards the living room, she took a seat while he poured them a whisky, his mind racing through possible scenarios. What the hell was she doing here? She must have walked, cold as she was—and in the dark no less. "Here."

"Thanks." Maggie took a long sip, her hands shaking until she wrapped them tightly around the glass. "I'm sorry for interrupting your night. I wouldn't have bothered ye if I could've avoided it."

He was about to ask her what happened, when he thought of all the other times he'd asked for an explanation and got nothing. It had his back going up. "I suppose ye can't tell me why ye're here or what has ye looking so scared."

Her gaze fell to her glass. "I didn't want to involve ye, Conall. And truth is, I couldn't. Still can't, but I think…" She looked up at him with weary eyes. "I think I'm going to anyway."

Part of him wanted to sit by her side and take her hand in his, and do what he could to comfort her. But there was another part of him that had him doubting her words and left him wondering if it was nothing but a lie to get him back. Not wanting to be a fool, he kept his distance and took the seat across from her, rather than by her side.

"So what's this about? What was important enough to ruin everything between us?" His hurt tainted his voice with bitterness, and he let it. If this was a game she was playing, then she should know the pain she was causing him.

"It's my brother." He scoffed, not at all surprised he'd be involved, when she continued. "Not Liam—Aidan. The older of the two ye met in Dublin."

He shrugged and took a sip of his whisky, thanking the gods for the fortification it offered, even if it was woefully inadequate. "What of him? He doesn't like me either, I suppose. Is that what this is about?"

She gritted her teeth and glared at him, anger aflame in those ice blue eyes. "Ye know, you can be a real arse sometimes."

"So I've been told." He knew he shouldn't be difficult with her, yet the hell she'd recently put him through left him in a less than amicable mood. "Well?"

She shook her head and got to her feet, her eyes shimmering with unshed tears. "Ye know—forget about it. It was a mistake to come here."

Stepping in her path, he grabbed her hand, his heart pounding against his chest. He cursed himself for being difficult with her when she was trying to open up to him. "It wasn't a mistake—I'm sorry for giving ye a hard time. Ye came here for a reason, and I want to hear what ye have to say. But I swear, Maggie, I need ye to be honest with me."

He steered her towards the sofa and, this time, sat by her side, pushing aside his uncertainties and reminding himself that she'd shown up at his door frightened. "So tell me about Aidan. Has he gotten himself into trouble?"

Maggie nodded, blinking hard to keep the tears from falling. It took some time, as if she were having some sort of argument in her head, leaving Conall to worry she'd back out before he got the explanation he so desperately needed. She leaned in and whispered on a trembling breath, "I'll tell ye everything, but please...do a sweep of the room to make sure it's secure. They might be listening."

He wanted to ask *who*? Who the hell was listening and what the hell had she gotten mixed up in? But he did as she asked with his heart racing, finally returning to her side, relieved to find his home hadn't been tampered with. "Now tell me. What the hell is going on, Maggie?"

She nodded her eyes, still shimmering ponds. "They've taken him. The Flahertys—Sean's family—are holding him hostage. It's why Sean's been in the area. To keep an eye on me."

He felt like he'd been waylaid, her words knocking the air out of him. It wasn't at all what he'd been expecting—and upset as she was, she had to be telling him the truth. No wonder she'd been out of sorts. And here he'd been thinking the worst of her. "What do they want?"

She shook her head and sighed. "What they want is an impossibility, which means I need to try to get Aidan free. Except that I don't know how. I've never dealt with anything like this."

So, she needed his help. He was nothing more than a way to get Aidan back—not that he could blame her when her brother's life was at stake. "Is that why ye came here? To ask for my help?"

"No." She chewed on her bottom lip as her eyes darted around. "It was Andrew. Liam and I were arguing."

"About?" Not that it was any of his business, but he was tired of not knowing what the hell was going on.

"Conall...I never wanted to keep any of this from ye. But from the start, Liam's been worried that involving ye would only make matters worse for Aidan—and he's probably right. Including you could be a deadly mistake." She ran a rough hand through her hair. "Anyway, I needed to clear my head so I went for a walk—heading in this direction out of habit. Then Andrew showed up in the middle of nowhere. "

He shook his head, confused, still too many questions to sort through. "What does Andrew have to do with this?"

"I'm starting to think he's been in on this from the start—maybe planted here by the Flaherty crew or persuaded to keep an eye on me." She looked distracted in thought, her entire body stiff. "I doubt it was a coincidence that we ran into Sean when we were in Dublin. Andrew must have overheard us mention we'd be heading over there—or maybe they had someone watching my parents' house."

It all seemed so surreal, yet the fear in her eyes when she'd pounded on his door and stumbled into his arms was real. And it had his protective streak flaring.

He cupped her cheek gently, her skin still cool to the touch. "And tonight? What did Andrew want from ye?" He swallowed hard, not wanting to think the worst, but needing to know. "Did he harm ye, Maggie?"

"No. Though I thought he might." She let out a ragged breath, her body so tense it was starting to shake. "It was all so odd. The way he showed up. I said I had to go—that you were waiting for me. He said he wanted to talk—that he had questions for me. When he grabbed my arm, I managed to twist out of his grasp. I just ran."

Images of what could have happened flooded his head, leaving him furious. He pulled her into his arms and held her close, trying not to think past comforting her. "We need to call the police."

She pulled away, her eyes wide with panic. "*We can't*, Conall. They'll kill Aidan."

"Whist, love." Cradling her against him, he moved them back to the sofa, as he tried to go through their options. "Then we need to figure out a way to get him back."

She sat back, looking weary and worried. "I'm not sure I should've involved ye. Things are complicated."

"What do they want in exchange for Aidan? I'm happy to help any way I can, but for fuck's sake, Maggie, ye need to be honest with me." He wasn't sure they could bring their relationship back to what it had been, but at least they'd be taking a step in the right direction.

She grabbed his hands. "You can't tell anyone, Conall—promise me."

"Aye, love. If I have yer honesty, then ye have my word." He searched her face, her eyes. "I need to know I can trust ye again."

"I never wanted to keep things from ye, Conall." She cupped his cheek, running her thumb over his lip, his breath hitching at her touch as his eyes slipped closed for a long moment. "You still mean the world to me."

"Then let's try to get yer brother back. Once we do that, we'll have a better sense of what's left of our relationship." As much as he loved her, the hurt she'd caused him had ripped open his old wounds and they wouldn't heal so readily this time around. "Now tell me what they want, love."

She took a deep breath and nodded, as if trying to steel herself. "They want the Hope. The necklace in exchange for my brother's life."

The breath went out of him like he'd been punched in the gut. "Och, Maggie…Ye can't."

She threw her arms up in exasperation. "Don't ye think I know that? It's why I couldn't tell ye what was happening. I didn't want to involve ye in such a thing. But this is my brother's life, Conall." When her voice cracked with those last words, he pulled her into his arms and held her.

"I know, love." Despite their problems, being able to hold her again had the tension in his chest slipping loose. "We'll figure something out, but…Maggie…we can't steal the jewels."

"We may not have to." She bit her bottom lip and let out a long breath. "If I can figure out a way to track down where they're keeping him, then maybe I can get him back. Then once he's safe, I can go to the authorities."

There were so many things that could go wrong, and if they did, it'd be Aidan's life on the line—and hers, if she was the one trying to steal her brother back. There may be an alternative, though. "Ye realize I can probably help ye track him down."

"I know…" She grabbed his hand and held it tightly. "But I don't want ye to think it's the only reason I'm here—or that it's the only reason I've finally come clean about what's going on. 'Cause it's not, love. I've wanted to tell ye all along. And I'm afraid there's more…"

How much more could there possibly be? "We've come this far, aye?"

"There's a reason the Flahertys have pulled us into this mess, and it has little to do with Sean being my ex." She looked down at her hands, and shook her head. "I should have told ye that night in Dublin when we were discussing out past. But I was too worried ye'd bolt if ye knew."

So she hadn't been completely honest with him even before her brother's kidnapping. It was yet another blow, and he felt himself pulling away once more, his defenses going up. "Just tell me, Maggie."

"It's my da. He used to run with the Flaherty crew—as a thief. High-end stuff. Paintings, jewels, anything they could sell to private collections for a pretty penny. He stopped ages ago, before I was even born and has never gone back to it." She reached out and took his hand. "I wanted to tell ye, but I know that reputation is everything in this industry and thought ye might rethink our relationship if your livelihood was on the line."

"Do ye really think I'd hold yer father's actions against ye?" He could understand her fears, but it still hurt to think she thought so little of him.

"I just didn't know if ye'd risk it, Conall. I know how important reputation is in the industry you're in, and worried you'd think twice about being with me if your livelihood was on the line. I was going to find a way to tell ye once we got settled back into our routine, but then we got word that they'd taken Aidan." Her eyes pleaded with him for understanding. They were so filled with hurt and worry, it left his anger warring with the part of him that wanted to ease her pain.

"I'll do what I can to help, but Maggie…" He closed his eyes and mustered his courage and strength, before facing her with a sigh. "We can't just pick up where we left off."

She pursed her lips together and nodded, her eyes shimmering with the tears she held back. "I know. And for that, I can't tell you how sorry I am."

"Och, love. Cheer up. It kills me to see ye so upset. We'll get yer brother back, aye?" He tucked a curl behind her ear. "But I need ye to stay positive."

She nodded, took a deep breath and then managed a smile, even if it looked forced. "You're right. We'll manage it somehow."

The scent of pork and spices was a sudden reminder that he'd left food cooking on the stove. "Shite."

He left her without a word and rushed into the kitchen, hoping he hadn't burned his dinner. Grabbing the spoon, he gave it a stir, the steam hitting him in the face as he sighed in relief, his dinner disaster averted.

"And here I was under the impression that ye don't cook." Maggie wandered in behind him, her hands stuffed into the pockets of her curve-hugging jeans.

He shrugged, and turned off the burner. "I don't care to, but I've got to eat something and eating out can get old."

"Well, that smells like there's far more effort and talent put into it than just *eating something*." She leaned against the counter with a hint of a smile that actually looked genuine this time. "I guess I'm not the only one who's been harboring secrets."

He shook his head, some of his anger dissipating. "Ye're not off the hook, Maggie. The fact that I can cobble together a meal when I said I didn't cook isn't the same as you not telling me about yer brother being abducted and yer father being a thief."

Gone was her smile. "I know that you may never be able to forgive me." He saw her struggle with the words—with the possible reality—before finding the strength to look him in the eyes. "But at least give yourself the credit you deserve, 'cause this smells damn good."

When she wandered closer, he scooped up a chunk of the simmering meat and handed her the spoon. She blew on it a few times, sending steam spiraling into the air, and then carefully took a bite. Her eyes went wide, and she slapped his arm, some of her old spunk coming back. "Ye're such a liar, Conall. That's amazing."

With a glare and pursed lips, he crossed his arms in front of his chest. "I suppose ye want to stay for dinner."

She shrugged with a hint of a smile. "If you're offering, I won't say no."

Bloody hell. Trying to keep his distance was going to be difficult. Especially when he'd done nothing but think of her since they split up. "I suppose it's easier than trying to get rid of ye."

Looking through a few of the cabinets, she found a couple of plates and set on the counter for him. "So what are we having?"

"Jasmine rice with spicy pork and pineapple." He dished it up. "Ye know, it's a good thing for you that this can only really be made in large batches and I wasn't cooking for one."

"A good thing, indeed." She looked up at him, her hand gentle on his back.

He stiffened and shrugged off her touch, his heart sinking and his emotions a tumultuous mess. By the gods, he loved her and yet he couldn't go there. "Don't, Maggie…I can't pick up where we left off like nothing happened. I'm happy to help ye get yer brother back, and I understand why ye did what ye did, but…it was a leap for me to trust ye, to let my guard down. I fell in love with ye, Maggie—and ye kept the truth from me. Ye pushed me away." And broke his heart. She had him questioning everything he thought he knew, he felt.

"I know I did, love—and for that I couldn't be any more sorry than I already am."

CHAPTER Seventeen

AFTER HASHING OUT a plan with Conall over dinner, Maggie rang up her brother and had him come over. Of course, Liam was none too happy about the plan, since they'd be taking a risk by straying from what the Flahertys wanted.

Maggie put her hand up to stop Liam's rant. "It's our best option. Would ye just hear us out?"

Glaring at them, Liam shifted his gaze and his anger between her and Conall. "If anything happens to Aidan, it's on *your* heads."

Her own anger flared, her hands clenching into fists as she took a step forward. "Not on our heads, Liam, but Flaherty's. Do ye hear me? This is no one's fault but theirs. And this is a far safer bet for getting Aidan back in one piece. The chances of us successfully stealing the Hope were never good. At least this way, we can find him—get him home safe."

"I can help track him down." Conall leaned against his kitchen counter, his long legs crossed at the ankle. "Even if his captors are using burner phones to make any phone calls when they're with Aidan, they'll likely still have their normal cell phones on them. That'll allow us to track their movements, which should help us figure out where they're keeping him."

Liam shook his head, his jaw clenched as he paced the kitchen, Piper nearly tripping him up on every other lap. "And how will ye get him back, yeah? What's the grand plan? Even if we know where he's being held, there's a good chance they'll put a bullet in his head before we get him out of there."

Maggie was happy to see Conall was still looking calm, rather than matching Liam's temper. They'd discussed the options and Conall's plan seemed the most feasible for getting Aidan back in one piece.

Conall shifted and ran a hand across his thick stubble. "Given the field I work in, I know a few people who might be able to help. I'll pull in a few favors and we'll see what they have to say on the matter. They've got more experience dealing with this sort of thing than all of us combined. And if it doesn't look like a good plan, then I'll speak to Iain about the necklace."

Liam spun on Conall. "And what exactly do ye think that'll accomplish? He's not going to just hand over the jewels, now is he?"

Things were getting tense and would only get worse if Maggie didn't step in her brother's path. "Would ye hear him out?"

With a nod of thanks in her direction, Conall continued explaining their secondary plan. "I've known Iain all my life—and he's a good man. He'd not want anyone coming to harm over some jewels."

Liam scoffed. "They're not just jewels though, are they? They're the bleedin' Highlander's Hope. A necklace of legend—the necklace said to bring Scotland its independence. Now, do ye really think he'll just hand them over?"

Maggie fought back her fears. She'd had the exact same thought, but Conall had convinced her Iain would be on their side. Now? She wasn't so sure. After all, it's not like Iain knew her in anything but a business capacity. It would be asking a lot, the risk for him enormous. Yet she had to believe. She had to keep her hope up. If she didn't, it'd be too easy to give in to her fears and let them cloud her judgment. Now more than ever, she had to stay positive. Had to believe things would get back to normal. Had to believe things would be all right.

She grabbed Liam's hand. "We'll only risk telling Iain if it looks like our first plan isn't going to work. In the meantime, we need to try to pretend that nothing's changed. We're still sticking to their plan to steal the jewels, as far as they're concerned."

"And what about the two of ye?" Liam tipped his chin in their direction. "I thought you were going to keep yer distance, Maggie."

"Whether I do or don't, it's none of yer business now that we've involved Conall in this mess. And keeping my distance will only make it harder for us to put a plan together and make it work." She bit back her anger. If Liam hadn't insisted on her pushing Conall away, they'd still be together. She should have trusted her gut from the start and known that Conall would be trustworthy and wouldn't do anything to jeopardize Aidan's life.

"Yeah, all right. I'll leave ye be." With hands on his hips and his head hung low, Liam sighed. "Just be careful, love. I'd never forgive myself if ye came to harm."

She slipped her arms around her brother's waist and gave him a hug as he kissed the top of her head. "I promise."

"And you." He let her go and tilted his head towards Conall. "I appreciate your help. Just do me the favor and take care of her—whether ye're together or not."

Conall gave her hand a squeeze and nodded, giving her a glimmer of hope. "I'll do my best—though ye know what she's like."

"I do. That's why I'm handing her off to ye. Anything happens to her, and me da will be skinning *your* hide, not mine." A crooked grin tugged at Liam's lips. "I'm off. Are ye coming?"

Good question. She knew Conall needed some space, yet she couldn't bear to leave him. Not yet, anyway. "I want to work out a few details. I won't be too long."

She could feel Conall's gaze shift to her. "And I'll make sure she gets home safe."

With Liam gone, they got to work. Maggie wrote down all the details she had on the Flahertys, in addition to all the information she had on the kidnapping itself, while Conall searched for information online. It was close to midnight and she should be exhausted, but she had enough work to keep her awake. She told herself it had nothing to do with the fact that she was spending time with Conall, who was working by her side.

He'd made it clear that he wasn't interested in picking up where they left off, and knowing what his ex put him through, she couldn't blame him. Not that she'd been much better, fully aware that she'd opened his old wounds. Guilt ate away at her, even though she told herself she'd pushed him away for his own good and to try to keep her brother safe.

Still…how could she not linger with the hope that, with time, he might learn to trust her again?

"Here, if ye'd like to have a look. I've mapped out all the properties owned and rented by the Flahertys, their kin, and known associates." Conall turned his laptop towards her and shifted closer, pointing to the screen. "There are a handful in Dublin, then a few more farther outside the city, and yet another, several hours away near Limerick."

She looked over the map, taking in the areas tagged with flags. "So how will we narrow it down? There are an awful lot of properties."

"I'm thinking they'd likely keep him close to Dublin, so they can come and go without too much trouble. Means we can probably get rid of the one in Limerick. But with the rest, they'd likely want something far enough out of the way so as not to be seen or…heard. If ye'd like to have a look, we can narrow it down and I'll start monitoring those areas for activity."

They wouldn't want to be heard because her brother might be yelling for help—or worse. She thought about the video, thought of his screams, and choked back a sob, turning away so he wouldn't see her so upset. "I'm sorry."

"Hey…what is it, love?" He ran a hand down her arm, making her want to lean against his touch for comfort, yet knowing she couldn't.

"There's a video of my brother. It might have clues to his location, but… I can't. I can't watch it again, Conall." She took a deep breath and then let it out slowly, her chest rattling as she exhaled.

He brushed her hair off her shoulder, his touch lingering. "Maybe we should call it a night. It's late, and we've got the weekend ahead of us to figure this all out. The video can wait until tomorrow."

"Yeah, you're right." Leaving him was the last thing she wanted to do, but she knew she couldn't stay. She ran her hands down her thighs as she got to her feet. "I'll see ye in the morning then? I could come by and take Piper on a run." Anything to see him again.

When Conall stood, Piper got up to follow with a yawn and a stretch. "I'll take ye home. And by all means, feel free to come get the pup. She's been missing ye."

No offer to stay the night, and it seemed as if Piper was the only one who didn't want her to go. "Thanks. I appreciate the ride, especially after running in to Andrew."

"What are ye going to do about him?" Conall's jaw tightened as he crossed his arms in front of his chest. "Because if you don't take care of it, I will."

"What exactly am I supposed to do? I can't exactly report him to the authorities for grabbing my arm and wanting to talk. And given everything that's going on, I probably just panicked for no reason." She grabbed her jacket off the back of the sofa and threw it on, before slipping her hands under her hair to free it from the fabric.

"Or he could be involved in this mess. What if he's the one who told Sean we'd be in Dublin? And the fact that he grabbed ye…" He shook his head, his jaw set tight with anger. "Whether we're together or not, I'll not have that man scaring and bullying ye—and I sure as hell won't have him manhandling ye."

At least he still cared enough to get angry on her behalf. And then she remembered the excuse she'd used when trying to get rid of Andrew. "Shite…I may have forgotten to mention a small detail."

His eyes narrowed in suspicion, making her heart beat all the faster. She loved how serious he could look. Loved the intensity of his gaze. Loved the intelligence that sparked in his eyes. "And what would that be with that guilty look on yer face?"

"I told him we were together to try to get him to leave me alone." She bit her lip and cringed. "He thought we'd broken up…"

"We have, Maggie."

She cringed some more. He was going to hate her. "I told him it was just a bump in the road, and we were back together—happy as Larry." She gave him a big hopeful smile. Maybe he would see the humor in it.

He sighed and shrugged out of his jacket, shaking his head. "Ye realize ye can't go home now, aye?"

"Why not?" Not that she minded much.

"Because if things are *happy as Larry* between us, then ye'd be spending the night. He could be watching the house, aye? Especially if he's working with the Flahertys. And it's *not* all right that he's gotten physical with ye, Maggie, and something will need to be done." He shook his head, looking exasperated.

She cringed. He'd never forgive her at this rate. It'd be impossible for her to screw things up worse than this. Not even if she tried. "I'm sorry, Conall. I can sleep on the sofa."

"And ye won't get a wink of sleep. There's a spare room next to mine. Ye can stay there."

Next to his? That certainly offered more potential than heading home. "I appreciate it."

B LOODY HELL. MAGGIE was going to be the death of him. Conall took a deep breath to try to settle the heat in his gut as she wandered into the kitchen for breakfast, sleep still clinging to her like fog on the heathers. Her hair was a wild tumble of gold and amber falling over her shoulder, so his gaze couldn't help but wander down to the precariously buttoned shirt she'd stolen out of his closet and those long, lean, naked legs.

"I see ye found one of my shirts." He poured them each a cup of coffee, hoping the distraction would be enough to keep him from lifting her up onto the counter and taking her then and there like a sex-crazed teenager.

"Hope you don't mind. I borrowed a pair of yer boxers too." She pulled up her shirt—his shirt—to show him, exposing the curves of her belly, the skin smooth over the firm muscles, the waist of his boxers hanging low enough to have his breath hitching and a ball of heat curling in his gut.

It was nearly impossible to ignore the effect she had on his body or the tension that shifted south. Taking a deep breath to steady himself, he handed her a coffee. "Here. Just the way ye like it—with far too much cream and sugar."

With a shrug of her shoulders, her eyebrows flicked up teasingly, her eyes alight. "Not like it's a big surprise that ye take yours black. So... what's for breakfast?"

"Ye'll have to pardon me for not setting out a buffet. I hadn't been expecting overnight guests." Knowing that she was asleep in the room next door to him had left him tossing around all night long. Sleep had refused to come as his mind raced through images from their time together, making it far too easy to picture her sleeping naked just feet away from him.

Best stick to the matter at hand. He may desperately want her, but he couldn't go down that road. He dug around for a pan. "I don't have a whole lot, but I do have a few eggs. Could manage crepes if ye're interested."

"I never say no to crepes. Although...from a man who supposedly doesn't cook? Not sure how good an idea that is." With humor in her eyes, she looked at him over her mug of coffee, holding it to her face with both hands.

At least she was in a better mood. So why did it put him on edge? Couldn't possibly have anything at all to do with the fact that he desperately wanted her, and she was making it damned difficult to keep his distance.

"Like I said, I can cook enough to keep myself fed." He grabbed the eggs and milk, and then dug around in the cabinet for the flour and sugar. "And by all means, if ye think you can do a better job, I'm happy to step aside and let ye have a go." He offered up the whisk, and then laughed when she didn't take it. "Thought so."

"I've got my own specialties." She leaned against the counter, facing him, with a teasing smile upon her lips and a mischievous glint in her eyes.

"Yeah…I've seen a few of those specialties, but they do little to fill an empty stomach." Bloody hell, she was making it so damned hard. Yet the last week and a half had been unbearable, and *she* was the one who'd put him through that hell, despite knowing his past. Clearly, there were extenuating circumstances, but it all came down to trust.

That's what hurt the most. She could have trusted him. She should have known he'd be on her side, not only to help get her brother back but to be there for *her*, so she wouldn't have to go through this alone. Instead, she hadn't thought him worthy. She'd lied and skirted the truth. Pushed him away and left him heartbroken. And she did all this knowing how difficult it had been for him to let down his guard and trust her.

No…she might be enticing, but he refused to be taken for a fool yet again. Not when his heart was on the line.

Once Liam arrived at Conall's, they got to work trying to track down where Aidan was being held. Conall also put in a call to his friend, Thorsen. He'd be a good one to have on their side, though there was a good chance he might be away on assignment. Having worked for Interpol, he was now an independent contractor, though what exactly he was doing these days, Conall would rather not know.

"There…the low ceiling and smaller window makes me think they're holding Aidan in an area that's more rural—an older home, similar to yer cottage, I'd think." Conall paused the video and then shifted out of the way so Maggie and Liam could have a closer look.

"Can you zoom in on the window? They have it covered over, but the thickness of the wall might give us an indication as to when the home was built." Maggie leaned forward for a better look, her body brushing against his as the three of them squeezed in around his desk. He did his best to ignore the nearness of her, but his body's reaction to her was immediate, leaving him wanton and longing for her.

He tried to push thoughts of her aside, and zoomed in on the image. "Just over a foot deep, I'd say."

Liam nodded and sat back. "The older cottages were built with walls more than two feet thick. I'd think this one here was probably built in the last seventy-five years."

Conall clicked over to the map he'd made up the night before with the marked properties around Dublin and just beyond. "I'll see if I can cross-reference the addresses I found last night with the year the buildings were built. With luck, we'll be able to narrow it down to just a few."

"And if ye're able to track their mobile phones, that'll help narrow it even further." She reached out and squeezed his hand for a brief moment, a small smile on her lips. "I can't thank ye enough for helping."

Starting his search on the homes, Conall gave her a shrug. "It's nothing ye couldn't have managed on yer own, though this is just the start of it. Things will get more difficult from here."

She bit her bottom lip. "Will ye still call your friend to help?"

"I already did, though I haven't heard from him yet. He's always good about getting back to me as soon as he's able, though, so I'm sure we'll hear from him before long." Conall copied the data to a new document, adding what other information he could find for each of the locations. "I'm going to be here a while with this, but can give ye a call once I have more information. Don't feel like ye have to hang around."

Not that he wanted to push her away, but he didn't trust himself. The more time he spent in her company, the more she wore down his defenses. The more he wanted to throw caution to the wind if it meant he could hold her in his arms.

Maggie didn't budge when Liam got to his feet. "I'll catch up with ye later. I have a few things I need to discuss with Conall, and if we're being watched by Sean or Andrew, then it's best we continue to keep up appearances that nothing has changed and we're sticking to their plan."

"Just keep in touch, yeah?" Liam looked from her to Conall. "I trust ye'll keep her safe?"

"I will." Though he was only putting his heart in jeopardy by not sending her away. Turning to her, he pinned her with a stare. "And we're working, ye hear?"

"Obviously. It's me brother's life that's at stake. What else would we be doing?" She shook her head as if he was daft.

"Later then. And Maggie—behave yerself. The man's helping us. Don't go harassing him." Liam gave her a warning look, but shook his head in defeat and then headed out the door.

"So, what can I do to help?" Maggie was already pulling out her laptop, the screen blinking to life.

"Since ye're familiar with the family, their friends, associates, it'd be helpful if you could jot down their names and start tracking down any information ye might think would be helpful." He wanted to have as much information gathered for Thorsen as possible.

She nodded and got to work, quietly tapping away beside him. Before long, the tension inside him eased as they each found their rhythm and things between them remained purely professional. After a while, he got up to stretch his legs and put the kettle on, making some tea and plating some biscuits. By the time he had the tea steeping, Maggie wandered in.

"Thank the gods—tea. I was starting to fade in there." She ran a hand over her face. "I might go out for a quick walk while the tea steeps. Exercise and cold air always helps wake me up."

After her run-in with Andrew, he wasn't sure he loved the idea. "Do ye think it's safe?"

"In broad daylight? I would hope so." She ran a hand down her arm as if warding off a chill. "You could come with me. Though I don't want to pull ye away from your work."

He could. Indeed, he *should* go with her. Yet he didn't want to upset the balance they'd found. It was nice to not constantly be tempted by her, and he had a sneaking suspicion that if they left work behind, he'd want nothing more than to put his heart on the line once more. "I have a few more things I want to check on, and I want to try Thorsen again. Ye won't be long?"

"No…" She threw him a small smile, despite the sigh that escaped those full lush lips. "Not long at all. I'll take Piper with me. She can pull a *Lassie* if I get into trouble."

"There's a better chance she'd be the one dragging ye over the cliff." He shook his head as visions of her demise flashed through his head. "Just be careful."

"I will."

Conall watched her go, doing his best to ignore that bounce in her step and that sweet behind. With a weary sigh, knowing his need would not be fulfilled, he sat down at his laptop with the list of names Maggie had jotted down. Starting with the immediate Flaherty family, he first crossed referenced their properties, and then moved on to tracking down their cell phone numbers. He sorted through the lists, but wanted to narrow it down further before attempting to track those people via their mobile phones.

Working with the list of addresses, he switched to a map of satellite and road views. If he could check out the building types at each given address, he might be able to match them to the cottage style they'd seen in the video. Pulling up one location after the other, he was quickly able to eliminate most of the buildings. There were, however, a few that might be the right style.

Logging in to his email, he found a message from Thorsen. Turns out his friend was closer than he thought. Not South America or the Middle East, but rather in Italy, helping to track and capture an art forger. Best of all, he was happy to come for a visit and help out in any way he could. Conall wrote him back and sent him the details, knowing his email line hadn't been compromised. It would be good to have Thorsen's help on this.

Conall checked the time. Maggie should have been back by now. Unless she took a longer walk than she'd anticipated, or lost track of the time. Yet it left him uneasy after her run-in with Andrew and with Sean still around. Conall called her phone, but it went through to voicemail. Not that it meant anything when coverage was so spotty in this area. Still, it was enough to have him grabbing his coat and heading for the door.

Not sure which way she'd gone, he turned in the direction they normally went when they took walks together. The wind coming in off the sea was brisk, the bite of it stinging his cheeks. His muscles tensed as he braced himself against the bitter chill, wondering why the hell Maggie hadn't turned back within minutes of stepping out. It only increased his worry that she'd been gone so long. He should have gone with her. Should have put aside his own worries and made sure she remained safe. If anything happened to her, he'd never forgive himself.

Digging out his phone, he tried her again. Still nothing. He lengthened his stride, his heart racing as he did his best to ignore the guilt that was eating away at him. He crested the hill and saw her off in the distance through the fog and mist. Relief washed over him—until the wind caught the fog and he saw a shadow shift not far from her.

He picked up his pace as she started to move towards him, the fog swallowing up anyone who may have been there. By the time he reached her, it felt like all the breath had been pulled from his lungs.

"I was worried about ye." Conall ran a hand down her arm, searching her face to make sure she was okay. "Who was that?"

Her smile faded as she looked at him with drawn brows. "I didn't see anyone. Was someone there?"

He looked around as if still expecting someone to come towards them. "I thought so, though I could be mistaken."

Looking worried, she glanced over her shoulder and moved closer to him, making him want to put a comforting arm around her. "Was it Piper or maybe the thick fog?"

He looked down at his wiggling dog, which was far too small to be mistaken for a man. It may have been nothing more than the mists, but the thought still bothered him. "I suppose it could have been the shifting fog. Let's get ye back. Ye must be frozen to the bone."

"I am. I swear it wasn't this cold when I left the house, and by the time the weather turned, we'd already wandered quite a ways." When she started walking back towards his home, he fell in step beside her.

The worry he'd felt had yet to fade, and he found himself reaching out to take her hand, despite all his previous hesitations. Few words were spoken as they walked back to the house, but by the time they got inside, he was frozen to the bone and was sure Maggie was in even worse shape.

Conall locked the door behind them. "How about I get a fire going, and then catch ye up on where we stand?" Leaning over, he gave Piper a good scratch before undoing her leash and hanging it by the door.

Maggie rubbed her hands over her arms, her cheeks and the tip of her nose flushed red from the cold. "Sounds perfect."

It didn't take Conall long to get a fire going, and given how cold Maggie looked, he made sure to build it up, tossing a few extra logs on for good measure. Already, he could feel himself thawing, the heat of the fire comforting. "Take a seat close by, and I'll grab the information I printed."

He handed her the information and then went to put the kettle on for more tea, the knot in his chest yet to dissolve. With Aidan's life at risk, the nagging guilt that he should warn Iain about the Flahertys, and most of all, his uncertain relationship with Maggie, he was on edge and there was little relief in sight. Not to mention he had Andrew and Sean to contend with.

He and Maggie were doing all that could be done to get Aidan safe, and with luck, the jewels wouldn't come into play. But regarding Maggie and how he felt about her…he'd never been more torn.

He told himself she'd be gone in a few months, anyway. With things uncertain between them, she'd have no reason to stick around. The thought pained him, but perhaps with her gone, it'd be easier to forget her and get back to his life. Easier to forget that she couldn't trust him, that she'd lied to him. Easier to heal. He'd gotten over Janet and he'd get over Maggie, too.

Suddenly weary, he poured the tea and steeled himself to be strong. Giving in to his feelings for her would only make it harder when she left. No good would come of it.

Putting up as much of a wall as he could manage in her presence, he headed back to the living room and handed her a mug. "Thorsen sent word. He's willing to help. Should be here in the next day or two."

"That's brilliant." Maggie was sitting cross-legged in front of the fire, and under normal circumstances he'd join her, but this time he grabbed his laptop and sat on the sofa. Not that it went unnoticed. She patted the floor. "Why don't ye come sit here and tell me about your friend?"

"Wouldn't know where to start. Thorsen is…unique. Ye'll like him, I think." He started typing away with the hope that she wouldn't notice he was still on the sofa. "Did ye have a chance to go through the addresses and homes? I'd like to have things narrowed down for him before he gets here."

She gave him a sly look, her elbows propped on her knees and a teasing smile on her lips. "Are you avoiding me, Conall? Because I get the distinct feeling ye are."

He glared at her over the top of his screen and then back at his keyboard, half wishing she'd just go away and leave him to his misery. "I know better than to bother with the impossible, and trying to avoid ye would be doing just that."

She pursed her lips. "Ye really know how to make a girl feel loved."

"I do try." Conall held her gaze, refusing to be lured by the sparkle in her eyes. She might be persistent, but he had a lot at stake and knew better than to give in to temptation.

"I get it, love. I really do." She let out a small laugh, but there was no humor in it. The sparkle faded from her ice blue eyes and her gaze slipped away from him, her shoulders slumped. "I know I no longer deserve yer trust—and for that I'm truly sorry."

She turned back towards the fire, picking up the printouts she'd been working with. A sharp pang of guilt haunted him, ripping at his resolve to stay strong. All he wanted was to comfort her—yet he still couldn't put his heart on the line.

"Maggie…I understand why ye did it—and I don't hold it against ye, love. But things are different now." He forced the air into his lungs, his chest so tight he could barely get a breath in.

He wished he could let it all go. Wished they could just pick up where they'd left off. Erase the last few weeks. Or start over. Yet the cursed tightness, his past, the hurt…they left him rooted to the spot, unable to move forward. "I'm the one who's sorry, Maggie. But there's nothing to be done for it."

Chapter Nineteen

With her focus on trying to get Aidan back, Maggie felt like she'd been neglecting her work at the museum. Between her troubles and the issues she kept running into on the site, she was falling behind and it bothered her to no end. At least work would help to keep her occupied now that Conall had left her heartbroken, though it did little to keep him from her thoughts. Even Liam had made himself scarce, doing his best to avoid her, though out of guilt or to escape her mood, she wasn't quite sure—nor did she care.

She spent the day finishing with the security measures she'd designed for the case that would house the Highlander's Hope. The glass casing would allow the necklace to be viewed from all sides—if she wasn't forced to steal it. She squeezed her eyes shut and ran her hands over her face. They'd get Aidan back. She had to believe that.

"Maggie, are you all right?"

She dropped her hands to her side and popped open her eyes, her heart already racing. "Andrew."

"Look, I'm sorry if I scared you the other day." He hung his head and stuck his hands in his pocket. "I wasn't thinking—girl alone in the middle of nowhere, guy she doesn't really know. I should've known better than to be so forward. My apologies."

Her anger flared, and this time, she was damned if she was going to show any fear. She wasn't sure if he had any connection to Sean, but it didn't matter. She wanted rid of him. "Look, Andrew. I don't know how many different ways I have to say it, but I'm not interested in you, and I'm no longer interested in being nice. You make me uncomfortable, and since my work and your work are separate from each other, we have no reason to interact—and that's exactly how I'd like to keep things."

"Ah." He flicked his eyebrows up and gave her a small smile. "I guess we've cleared that up now. Not interested. Got it. And you're with Conall, anyway. Right?"

"Don't know how that's any of yer business." He clearly wasn't convinced but she didn't care. Not one bit.

She watched him wander off and got back to work, but the interaction had left her jittery and on edge, her focus shattered. With the end of the workday approaching, she wrapped up and headed to the bus to see where Liam stood with his project. A pang settled around her heart, knowing that if she was still with Conall, she'd be getting ready to head over to his home. They'd be having a bit of dinner and a pint, and then spend the rest of the evening in each other's arms.

Instead, she'd be home with one brother while worrying about the other.

Liam put down his soldering iron, and looked up at her. "I think I'm going to head to the pub and see if Sean's there. Do ye want to come?"

"Why the hell would I want to deal with that bastard?" She shot him a look like he'd lost his mind.

"Ye know how he gets if he starts drinking. I'm hoping he'll drop his guard and say something—anything—that could help us find Aidan. Might even pass out long enough for me to have a look at his phone." He gave her hand a quick squeeze. "It's worth a try, right?"

"It is." She dropped into the seat next to him. "You're better off going without me. I won't be able to hold my tongue, and it'll be too tempting to stick a knife in the bastard and send his head home."

"Believe me when I tell ye, I've had the same exact thought." He grabbed his coat and got to his feet. "Don't wait up."

"Just be careful, yeah? The last thing I need is to have two of ye missing or in trouble with the Flahertys. The whole lot of them might be arses, but they're smart and they're ruthless. Don't forget it, Liam."

"I won't, love."

By the time Maggie made it home, she wanted nothing more than to crawl under the covers. She picked through the leftovers in the fridge, knowing she'd be starving at midnight if she didn't eat something. Yet with everything that was going on, her normally healthy appetite had dwindled to nothing. While the tea steeped, she made herself a grilled cheese sandwich after deciding she wasn't in the mood for roast chicken or beef stew.

Taking her dinner into the living room, she turned on the TV, hoping it would distract her from worrying about Aidan and missing Conall. Her mind kept replaying the way Conall touched her, kissed her, the way his body fit so perfectly with hers. And how she'd hurt him with her lies, ruined what they had between them, lost the man she loved.

Her last heartache had been hard—had left her devastated and depressed—but it was nothing compared to how she now felt now that she'd lost Conall. She could feel the darkness closing in around her, and tried her best to push it back. Tried to focus on getting over him.

Conall had made it abundantly clear that things couldn't go back to the way they were, and she understood why, even if it left her heartbroken.

He'd taken a huge leap of faith with her, offered her his honesty, his trust and his heart. And she'd repaid him with lies.

Her eyes stung with tears, yet she couldn't let the darkness take over. If she gave in to it, if she showed weakness, it would swallow her whole, and she didn't think she'd ever emerge from it. She had to be strong. Had to focus on the positive. Focus on living each day to the fullest. Even if every breath was taken with a broken heart.

She took another half-hearted bite of her sandwich, washed it down with tea, and was debating between watching a movie or calling it an early night when her cell rang.

Conall. Shite.

She debated not answering it, but Conall didn't usually call just to chat, which meant he likely needed her for something. With a deep breath, she steadied herself and answered the phone. He was brief, as usual. His friend Thorsen had arrived and had questions for her. About Aidan. With her heart racing, she hung up and grabbed her jacket.

Conall opened the door before she had a chance to knock, her arrival most likely given away by Piper's excitement and barks. He gave her a hesitant smile that made her pulse race and her heart ache for him. "Thought ye might want to be here from the start."

She hung up her jacket and put her bike helmet down on the bench by the door, her emotions running high, the more it sunk in that things were over between them. She gave the pup a scratch, trying to settle her mood and gather her strength before turning to face Conall. "I appreciate the call—and the help. I know you're going out of your way and it means a lot."

As his gaze took her in, searching her face and her eyes, his lips turned down in a pout. "Are ye all right?"

She let out a laugh of exasperation, though she kept her voice down, knowing Thorsen was in the other room. "How the hell am I supposed to be all right? My brother could easily turn up dead, I'm being pressured to steal a priceless treasure and put my career on the line, and I finally manage to forget my past heartache and fall in love again, only to have it all go to hell and have my heart broken again. My life is completely banjaxed. So *no*, Conall. I'm not all right, and don't think I will be for quite some time."

She squeezed her eyes shut and pinched the bridge of her nose. She was such a fool. What was she doing? What was she thinking? She should have kept that mouth of hers shut.

"Och, Maggie…" He ran a hand down her arm but she shrugged it off, knowing she'd only want to melt into his arms. She'd already made enough of a fool of herself. She didn't need to make it any worse.

"I'm sorry. I shouldn't have said anything." She forced herself to look into his eyes and smile. "We've left yer friend waiting, and after he's come all this way to help. He'll be wondering what's the matter."

"Maggie…" His brow furrowed, only adding to his look of concern. "I'm sorry if I've only added to yer pain. I wish matters were different between us. I really do."

"I know, Conall. Ye can't trust me. I get it." Her shoulders slumped with a sigh as her eyes burned. "Can we just go talk to Thorsen? The sooner we do, the sooner I'll be out of ye hair."

"Don't go making it sound like I find ye a nuisance, when ye know that's not the case." His jaw tightened as he gave his head a shake. "And what happened to pretending we're a couple? I thought ye wanted to keep up appearances."

"I don't know that it matters. I ran into Andrew today and I get the impression he knows it's nothing but a lie. So what's the point? I'm miserable enough without the constant reminder that things are over between us." It was overwhelming her to be so close to him and to know it was over, to know there was no convincing him otherwise.

Anger sparked in his eyes as he took a step closer. "Was he harassing ye again? I think it might be time I had a talk with him."

"I took care of it, Conall." It was nice that he cared enough to get angry on her behalf, but she didn't want to drag him into any more of her messes. "I've caused ye enough problems already. Now, please…can we just try to get my brother back?"

Conall ran a rough hand through his hair, his head hung low. "Aye, love. As ye wish. Come, then."

As they moved into the living room, Maggie's gaze immediately fell on the man who was getting to his feet. Though she hadn't given Thorsen much thought, she was caught off guard by his looks and presence. She didn't know what he'd been doing for Interpol, but she doubted being inconspicuous had been in his job description. There was no way the man standing before her could go unnoticed, even if he tried. He looked like a Viking hankering for a fun pillage and raid.

The first thing that caught her attention were those eyes. The color of a tropical lagoon, they held her captive, making it difficult for her to turn away. He was also *very* tall and muscular, but in a way that made her think he could still move lightning fast and that those big, strong hands of his could be deadly—or absolutely perfect. Add to that a smattering of light freckles, ginger stubble over a strong jaw and longer hair worn loose, and she'd be swooning—if Conall hadn't broken her. Broken her heart and killed any interest she might normally have in a man.

Before Conall, she would've happily flirted and teased and hopped into bed with the man—should he be willing. Yet now? All she could do was long for Conall's touch.

Thorsen reached out and shook her hand, his smile totally disarming, so she couldn't help but forget some of her troubles and smile back. "I'm Thorsen. It's a pleasure to meet you, though I wish it was under more pleasant circumstances."

"Maggie. And the pleasure's mine. I can't thank ye enough for coming all this way to help get my brother back and on such short notice, too. I don't know how I'll ever repay ye." With her hand still in his, she felt a heat flush her cheeks.

"I'm just happy to help. It's not every day I can come to the aid of a pretty lass." They all took a seat as Thorsen continued with a tilt of his head towards Conall. "We took another look at the video and the information you've gathered. They seem to have a fair amount of experience being criminals, but I'd venture to say that they haven't done a whole lot of abductions."

"So what does that mean for getting my brother back?" Maggie wasn't sure if she should be scared or relieved.

Conall took her hand in his and gave it a squeeze. "Thorsen thinks he can pull in the connections he has and not only get yer brother out of there safely, but could also bring down the Flaherty crew so they'll not be bothering ye again."

Hope mingled with relief, even if they were tentative. It was the closest she'd come to possibly getting her brother back. "I can't thank you enough—both of ye. If there's anything I can do to help—if there's anything ye need—just say the word."

Conall looked at their linked hands, and then, as if remembering himself, let go, sending another pang straight to her heart. "There's a good chance we'll need to tell Iain. Thorsen's connections might need the jewels—or something that looks an awful lot like them—if they're going to try to make a trade."

"I guess we'll have to." She'd been hoping to avoid telling Iain.

Though she didn't have many options before she'd confided in Conall, she couldn't get away from the fact that she would have stolen the jewels if there hadn't been another way to get her brother back. She felt horrible about it. Not only because she'd always led an honest life, despite her father's early ventures into thievery, but because this could now ruin her hard-earned reputation. Still…she'd sacrifice it all for her brother, and with luck, Iain and Cat would understand.

"Dinnae fash, love. Above all, Iain puts family first." Conall swept a stray curl from her eyes, his touch lingering. "He'll not hold it against ye, and we'll only tell him if it becomes necessary to the plan."

It took all she had to not lean into him, and it was killing her that he kept doing this to her. It was hard enough for her to keep her distance, let alone when he kept touching her. Yet he was the one pushing her away. He was the one who wanted to end things. He was the one who couldn't trust her or give her another chance.

She was tempted to show him what it would be like if she were no longer his. No longer in his life. No longer his to touch and hold. Maybe then he'd realize that he'd made a mistake and what they had was worthy of another shot. Yet she wasn't one for playing those sorts of games. She just had to find the strength to move on, and once she did, that would be it. She'd lock away the love she'd felt for him and bury it deep. It was her only defense against a broken heart.

"So, what do we do next? I desperately want this nightmare over with and my brother back." She forced herself to focus on the task at hand, so she'd be less tempted to fall into Conall's arms. "My parents are beside themselves."

Thorsen gave her a reassuring smile. "I'm thinking it might be easiest to just go in covertly and raid the place rather than try to trade the necklace. I'm working on putting together a team that specializes in this sort of thing. It'll be your brother's best bet for getting out of there safely. Time is of the essence whenever there's a hostage involved, so I'd like to think my contacts will be moving on this pretty quick. It helps that the Flahertys are known to the authorities. It's been hard to get enough evidence to press charges, and this would be enough to bring them down."

"They said not to involve the police. Are you sure this is safe? And the cost…I don't know how quickly I could get the funding to pay your team." Not that she had many other options.

Thorsen nodded with a reassuring smile and confidence that set her at ease. "Interpol's happy to finally have something against the Flahertys, so they're taking care of the cost. As for the team, they specialize in this sort of thing. The Flahertys won't know what hit them until it's too late."

She nearly burst with relief. "I can't believe this nightmare could soon be over."

Conall gave her a small smile that lit his amber eyes from within. "Aye, love. Maybe then things will get back to normal for ye."

Except she didn't want to return to the life she'd led before coming to Dunmuir. Not when that life didn't include Conall.

CHAPTER
Twenty

C ONALL TOOK A long draw from his pint, happy to have talked
Maggie into joining them for dinner, even if he should be trying
to distance himself from her. He just couldn't quite manage it,
always drawn to her like fog to the heather.

Not wanting to run into Sean for fear he might wonder about
Thorsen and get suspicious, they opted to go out to dinner in one of the
neighboring towns. It was a nice little gastro-pub he'd been intending
to bring Maggie to when they were still together.

He threw her a sideways glance, as his heart attempted to overrule his
head, leaving him still longing for her. Even Thorsen seemed smitten by
her charms—and he was always a hard one to impress.

A pang of jealousy sparked in his chest as Maggie laughed at one of
Thorsen's stories, and Conall poked at his perfectly cooked steak. He

should be happy that she and his friend were getting along. And he was—as long as their getting along didn't turn to flirting. Or worse.

Not that he had any claim. Maggie could do whatever she wanted, with whomever she wanted to do it with, and truth be told, Thorsen was a great guy. It made no difference that he still had feelings for her if he wasn't going to pursue them—if he was going to let her go.

As beautiful and smart as she was, she'd not remain single long. That was for sure. So why not be happy that she'd at least be hooking up with someone he knew would treat her right?

A gentle hand on his arm pulled him from his thoughts, as he looked up into Maggie's kind eyes. "Are ye all right? You were scowling at your steak like it'd gone and *moo'd* at ye."

"Sorry. Just distracted." He shook his head to try to clear it. Maybe if he turned the conversation back to getting Aidan home, it'd keep their flirting and his jealousies to a minimum. He turned his attention to Thorsen. "Will ye need us to head to Dublin with ye?"

Thorsen shook his head as he took a long draw from his pint. "No. I want you to continue going about your business as if nothing has changed. I've got a room booked not far from here for tonight so as not to draw any attention and then will head to Dublin come morning. With luck, this will all be over in just a day or two. We'll get your brother back to you, Maggie."

"I can't believe it and can't thank ye enough." Her smile reached her eyes, making them sparkle as Maggie reached across the table and grabbed Thorsen's hand, giving it a squeeze. It was for no more than a moment, but it still had Conall second-guessing himself.

She turned to him, just a heartbeat away, her gaze locked on his as she took his hand and held onto it. "And you—I owe ye everything, Conall."

He wanted to kiss her. Desperately. To hold her face in his hands and kiss her until there was nothing else, until everything around them fell away. Yet pushing her away these last few weeks now left him with a wall up and he was having one hell of a problem tearing it down. And by all accounts, she could see it in his gaze. Sorrow and disappointment glazed over her ice blue eyes as she let go of his hands, her shoulders slumping before she looked away.

Thorsen looked over at him, his brows drawn together in question. Conall sighed and shook his head. He was sure Thorsen would grill him once they were alone.

Damn it. He cursed himself for being such an arse. She was one big step closer to getting her brother back. She was happy. And she loved him. Yet he was being a fool and a bastard, upsetting her when she finally had some hope.

The rest of their dinner was spent with Maggie saying barely a word, and everyone's good mood stifled. By the time they got back to his house, Maggie was already looking to leave. "I've got work to do. If you could just keep me updated on what's going on with my brother, I'd appreciate it."

Thorsen gave them some space, deciding he'd take the dog out. The moment they were alone, Conall grabbed her hands. "Stay just a wee bit longer, Maggie. I'm sorry if I've been difficult."

She sighed and gave his hands a squeeze. "Ye haven't been difficult, Conall. Not at all. I mean, I'm going to be getting my brother back and that's because of you. It's not yer fault things didn't work between us. Ye have every right to be tentative after all ye went through with Janet."

He chewed on his bottom lip as his mind and heart raced to decipher the tumult of emotions and thoughts running through him. Things were suddenly feeling very final between them. "Still…I wish it could be different."

She shrugged. "Like I've said, ye have to live your life to the fullest. There's no point on wasting your energy on a relationship that won't work for ye. But…Conall, this is it. If ye turn me away now, it's truly over between us. I love ye with all my heart, but I can't waste my life away pining for ye. This is your last chance."

"'Cause life's too short." It felt like his heart was in a vise. He should take another chance on her. On them. Yet he couldn't get the words out, the pain and heartache preventing him from speaking the words that would keep her from leaving. "I love ye, Maggie. Surely ye know that."

Her eyes shimmered with unshed tears, yet she stood tall, her gaze locked on his. "And yet it's still over, isn't it?"

"I wish it wasn't, love."

Conall nursed his drink as Thorsen shook his head, his jaw slack with disbelief. "Conall…you're the smartest man I know, yeah? But I've got to tell you, you're being a goddamned idiot."

"You of all people know what I went through with Janet. I was hesitant to get involved with anyone at all, but took a chance with Maggie, only to have her lie to me. She couldn't trust me even though she knew I might be able to help. Can ye really blame me for not wanting to get burned again?" Conall took another long swig of his whisky, annoyed with himself and the situation he was in. Why the bloody hell couldn't anything be simple. A kidnapping! Of all the things to sabotage his relationship.

"But Maggie isn't Janet. Not by a long shot." Thorsen sat forward, folding his long frame in half as he propped his elbows on his thighs. "And if her brother's life is on the line, then you have to cut her some slack. It's not like she'll have dealt with that sort of situation before."

"I get it, Thorsen. I really do. I understand why she did it, and I don't blame her for it. But…" Conall ran a rough hand through his hair and down his face. "But I feel like there's this huge chasm between us now, and I can't for the life of me figure out how to cross it."

"Well, you better figure out how to build a shagging bridge before it's too late and she's gone for good. 'Cause let me tell you, she's not going to stay single for long. Hell…you're just lucky you're like my brother." He shook his head, wearing a crooked smile. "A girl like Maggie? Smart, sweet, and gorgeous? Wars have been started over women like her."

"It doesn't matter, one way or another. She's moved on. She gave me one last chance and I turned her away." Speaking the words out loud left him feeling like he'd just been given a death sentence, not quite believing he'd done such a fool thing. "I really do wish I could find some way of making it work, but—"

"But nothing, man." Thorsen's lips were pursed into a thin line, anger sparking in those blue eyes. "You're being a fool, Conall. Pull your head out of your arse and figure it out. Figure out a way to get past whatever's holding you back, 'cause I can tell you now, this will be a regret that will haunt you the rest of your life. It's not too late, but for fuck's sake, don't drag your feet on this or she will be gone—gone for good, and you'll have ruined any chance you have at happiness."

It felt like the earth had crumbled out from under him, and he was suddenly falling into a black abyss. *Maggie*...What the hell had he done? A fool indeed.

And yet…

Conall took a deep breath and held it until his lungs burned. "Let's get her brother back safely first. Then I'll speak to her about trying to make things work between us."

"And you don't think it'll be too late by then?" Thorsen shook his head, still looking at him like he was an idiot. "You're taking a risk, Conall. But hey, it's none of my business. Just know that if she's still available a month from now, she's fair game as far as I'm concerned. I might have a fool for friend, but it doesn't mean I'm daft. Not when Maggie's the prize."

Despite knowing that his friend was trying to spur him into action, his jealousy flared. "Ye really know how to push my buttons, Thorsen."

Thorsen shrugged, his lips curled into a goading smile. "So? What are you going to do about it?"

With Thorsen off to Dublin to help get Aidan back, Conall couldn't help but mull over his friend's words. He loved Maggie. Of that he had no doubt. And Thorsen was right. Maggie was nothing like Janet and the circumstances were extreme. Whatever had been holding him back, whatever tore them apart—he couldn't let it continue to come between them. She was too important, and it wouldn't be long before she moved on. If she hadn't already done so.

Her words now haunted him and a panic settled in his gut, spurring him on to find her. It had been less than a day since she'd asked him one last time if they could make it work. Less than a day since he'd turned her away. Less than a day—and somehow it felt like he was already too late. Like that day may as well have been an eternity.

He drove to the cottage, but there was no one there, so he tried the bus and found Liam. Still no Maggie, though.

Liam shook his head as he propped himself against the doorjamb, his jaw tight even when he spoke. "Look, I appreciate your help in getting Aidan back, but just do us all a favor and stay clear of Maggie. She's trying to get over ye and will manage it just fine, but only if you're not trying to confuse her. She deserves better than to have her head and heart messed around with."

"I'm not toying with her, Liam. And I need to talk to her." Conall tried not to get frustrated. He knew Liam was just trying to protect his sister, no different than what he would do as a big brother. "Things went wrong between us, but I'm here to do right by her."

"Yeah? Well, good luck with that," Liam scoffed with a shake of his head, making Conall wonder if he was indeed too late. "She said it was over between ye—and I hate to tell ye, *laddie*, but that doesn't bode well for your chances if ye now think you can get her back. Once she moves on, she does just that."

Conall swore under his breath, and tried to stay calm. He'd make her see sense. He had to. 'Cause he couldn't live with the alternative. "I don't suppose ye know where she's gone to?"

"Nah. Didn't say, though she took off on that bike of hers. Said she needed a distraction." Liam ran a hand across his stubbly jaw. "May have headed to Glasgow. There's a pub she likes to frequent when we're in the area and she's looking to get herself into a bit of trouble. The Dun Cairn, I believe."

"That's nearly two hours away." The woman was mad. Certifiable to be going there on that deathtrap of a bike, with dark approaching and the roads almost always slick with wet. And the thought of her looking for a bit of trouble set him on edge, knowing exactly the sort of distraction she might be looking for. "If she calls or shows up, I'd appreciate it if ye had her call me."

Liam shook his head with a sigh. "I'll tell her."

He sat in his car and tried her cell. With any luck, she stayed closer to Dunmuir rather than venturing all the way to Glasgow, since news of her brother was imminent. Not that he could get through to her. Maybe she decided to head into town for a pint. It'd be easy enough to spot her bike, and with a renewed hope of finding her, he pulled out onto the road and drove towards town.

He didn't get that far. Her bike was parked on the side of the road near the trail that led to the standing stones. Pulling in behind her bike, he parked his car and got out, the cold wind whipping around him as it came in off the sea. He followed the trail as it snaked its way through the heather and up to the crest of the hill where the ancient stones stood.

When he found her sitting on an outcropping of rocks, he let out the breath he'd been holding, some of the tension in his chest easing even if the hardest part was still ahead of him. "Maggie."

"Hey. It's not about Aidan, is it?" She bit her bottom lip, her brow furrowing as her eyes darkened with concern.

"No. I've yet to hear from Thorsen. Perhaps tonight or tomorrow." He sat down next to her, his heart tripping out an uneven rhythm. By the gods, he hadn't been this nervous in a long time. "Can we talk?"

She shrugged with a sigh. "What is there to say, love? Ye've made yerself abundantly clear and ye need not worry. I just need to get Aidan back, and then I'll be out of your hair in the upcoming week. I'm nearly done with most of the security, and Liam will stick around to wrap up the tail end of things."

It felt like a punch to the gut. She was leaving. In less than a week she'd be gone. He could barely get the words out past the fear of losing her. "Don't go, Maggie. I made a mistake, and for that I'm sorry. I want things to go back to the way they were."

She shook her head with a laugh, though there was no humor in it. "If only it were that simple, love."

CHAPTER
Twenty One

MAGGIE FELT NUMB. She should be ecstatic—Conall wanted her back. So why did it still feel like it was over between them? One deep breath after another, she took in the cool and pungent sea air, hoping it would help calm her, hoping it would slow her racing thoughts. She pressed her palms against the rough rock they were sitting on, hoping to ground herself in the ancient place, as if the wisdom of the centuries might aid her in her plight. Yet the voices of the old ones were silent, nothing but a thrumming that rode on the cold wind, their whispers offering up nothing.

Conall took her hand in his, making her heart ache with a desperate pain that threatened to overtake her. She pulled her hand from his, shaking her head and not quite believing she was going to push him away.

"I can't do this, Conall. *I can't.* You weren't the only one taking a chance. You weren't the only one taking a leap of faith with this relationship. My brother was kidnapped, damn it." She swiped at the tears that escaped down her cheeks. "You'd think, given the circumstances, that ye'd see past my mistakes. I needed a bit of understanding and did all I could to make things good between us. Yet ye still turned me away."

He cupped her face in his hands and brushed the tears from her cheeks. "Och, love. I know. I've been an arse. But…I love ye, Maggie."

"I get that it was hard for you to trust me, but in the end, you threw up yer hands and walked away from what we had. So what about the next time there's a problem between us? Will ye walk away then? 'Cause I need someone who'll stick around, Conall, through thick and thin—and I'm not sure that's you."

"That's where ye're mistaken. And I'll prove ye wrong if ye'll just let me." He shook his head, his eyes pleading with her. "We both made mistakes, love. And it would be yet another mistake—the biggest one of all—if we didn't give this another try."

Still holding her, he brushed his lips against hers and kissed her until her objections faded, her pulse racing just under her skin. He left her dizzy and wanton, her heart aching for him like it had never done for any other. His kiss deepened and she melted into him, her heart pushing out all logical thought, all warnings. She could do no more than lose herself in him, in his touch, in his kiss.

Her head dropped back as he tangled his fingers in her hair and nipped down her jawline to her neck, her chest pressing against his muscular form with each breath. When he spoke, his words were but a whisper against her skin, her lips. "I love ye, Maggie. With all that I am, I love ye."

She pulled away enough to look into those gold eyes of his. "And I love you, Conall. But…" She took one last kiss and then put some distance between them, her head swimming with uncertainty and confusion. "I just don't know if I can do this." Her voice cracked on those final words—as did her heart.

He shook his head, his jaw set tight. "I'm not letting ye go, Maggie. I was a fool once, but I'll not be a fool again. Ye can't just give up on us, love."

"It was you who gave up on us, damn it." She wanted to pound on his chest, frustration and hurt knotting up her insides.

His cell phone rang, the sound of it nearly swallowed by the wind. He held onto her a moment more, before pulling away to dig his phone out of his pocket. "It's Thorsen."

Conall answered it as Maggie's heart pounded away, her muscles knotted with tension. He said little, listening instead, the few words he'd spoken giving little indication as to what was being said. So many things could go wrong.

He hung up. "At this point, the plan is that they'll raid the place in the wee hours of the morning. They figure that'll be their best bet for getting yer brother out of there safely. Things might change if they see an opportunity, but Thorsen will do his best to keep us updated."

She pulled herself away from her emotions, and concentrated on what was important—getting her brother back. "You should know—and ye'll probably want to tell Iain as well—but I believe that Andrew is indeed working with Sean. My brother went looking for Sean last night, hoping that with a few pints, Sean might slip up and give something away to help find my brother. He saw him talking to Andrew down one of the alleys. Makes me wonder if Andrew may have also been responsible for all those problems on the site, the mangled wires, the alarm on my bus being set off." It might not be him, but Maggie doubted it.

"Well, ye've suspected him for a while now." With a shake of his head, his lips pursed with annoyance. "I knew that bastard was up to something. From the very start, something felt off about him."

She managed a small laugh, happy she could still do so. "Are ye sure it wasn't just jealousy?"

"Ye can't blame me for wanting to keep ye to myself when ye're my very heart." He cupped her cheek, his eyes locked on hers, his gaze so intense she struggled to not look away. "I want ye back, Maggie. We belong together."

"And last night? Did we not belong together then when you turned me away?" She wanted nothing more than to fall into his arms and wipe the slate clean, but she was annoyed and frustrated and hurt. "How could ye give up on us so easily—especially once ye knew the circumstances?"

"Och, love. I hadn't given up. And ye're right to be angry with me. I was letting my past get in the way of following my heart. I only hope ye can find it in ye to forgive me for being such a fool." His fingers brushed her cheek, his eyes still on hers, holding her heart and soul captive. "I love ye, Maggie, and that never ceased to be the case."

She could feel her defenses melting, but still managed to hold her ground. "I'm not ready to take ye back, Conall. Ye broke my heart." Yet there was one more truth she needed to face. "And what if we're too alike—too broken from our pasts and ready to run just so we won't get hurt again?"

"I'm not going anywhere, love—and neither are you. I'm committed to making this work, because I know there's no one else who'll ever make me as happy as you do. I just need ye to give me—give us—another chance." He dropped his forehead to hers, cupping the back of her neck, his breathing ragged with emotion. "I'm begging ye, Maggie. Let me prove to ye that I'm worthy of yer love."

She shook her head in frustration, annoyed that she was having such a hard time staying angry with him. He'd made his decision, damn it, and as a result, she'd made hers. And yet...she knew he was right. She couldn't imagine ever being happy with anyone but Conall. "Ye're a pain in the arse. Ye know that, right?"

He smiled and kissed her, his eyes alight. "Aye, love. I know. And yet ye love me anyway."

Forcing her emotions away, she put a finger on his chest and pushed him back, her gaze stern. "You being a pain in the arse does *not* mean I'm taking ye back, Conall."

"Wouldn't dream of it." With a smile, he brought her hand to his lips. "What if ye keep me company while I wait for Thorsen to call with an update? That way ye'll have the information as soon as he rings. Given how spotty cell service is around here, ye might not want to chance being in a dead zone when he calls."

He wasn't making it easy for her to walk away, knowing that if she stayed in his presence, she'd have a hard time not succumbing to his charms and her heart. Still…it was news about her brother. "Only if ye make those crepes of yours—and ye keep your distance. I'm not daft, Conall. I know this is nothing but one of yer ploys."

When he laughed out loud, his smile only made her want him more. "My ploys? Ye make it sound like I'm a schemer. And maybe I am, since I'd do anything to make ye love me once more. Anything to make ye stay." His mood turned serious, his smile fading. "Ye can't leave in a week's time, Maggie. Not when there are so many reasons for you to stay."

She had to look away, helpless to keep the tears from falling, the rollercoaster ride of emotions taking their toll. "I never stopped loving ye, Conall. You know that."

"Aye. Just like ye know that I never stopped loving you."

CHAPTER
Twenty Two

CONALL COULDN'T BEAR to think he might lose her. If she left, it'd be impossible to convince her to give him one more chance. Still…she had yet to go. There was still time to change her mind.

His eyes wandered over the ancient stones, his gaze lingering on the one with a hole in its center. For thousands of years, lovers had used it to declare their love, their hands passed through the opening and their promises spoken, linking their hearts and souls together as one. It was all he had—a bridge for the chasm. "I swear it on the lover's stone—ye're my everything, Maggie. The blood in my veins, the air I breathe. Without you, nothing else matters, my love. I'm asking ye for a chance to make things right between us."

She cupped his cheek as her eyes searched his face and sent his heart racing. He couldn't help but lean into her touch, turning to kiss her palm. Gently, she pulled her hand away. "We should go."

"Aye, we should." He managed a smile, refusing to let disappointment set in. She hadn't given him an answer—but that also meant she hadn't turned him away. There was still hope. "Ye wanted crepes, right? Why don't we do that then? It'll also give me a chance to check my email to see if Thorsen's sent anything."

They got back to his home just as the sun was setting, the sky painted in pinks and blues. The last of the day's light poured through the large windows that flanked his fireplace. It didn't take long to get a fire going, and after being out in the brisk wind, the warmth of it was comforting.

"I got ye a whisky. I don't like to drink alone, and right about now, I need a drink." Maggie handed him a glass and propped herself against the arm of the leather sofa, watching him toss a few more pieces of wood on the fire, sparks dancing on the heat as they floated up to die as ash.

He stood and turned towards her, taking a long sip from his glass before reaching over and giving her hand a squeeze, knowing how worried she was about her brother. "Dinnae fash, love. Thorsen's good at what he does. He'll make sure Aidan gets back to ye safe."

She nodded and looked down at her drink, but Conall could see all her emotions riding just under the surface of her delicate skin, even if she was doing her best to hold it together. "What if something goes wrong? What if he's hurt in the process?"

"Och, love. Ye've got to stay positive." He pulled her to him and cradled her head against his shoulder, his own heart aching to see her so upset when there was little he could do but be there for her. "Let's get ye fed, aye? It's hard to find hope on an empty stomach."

Grabbing the ingredients he'd need, he decided to try to distract her from her worries. "Come on. I'm going to teach ye how to make crepes."

Her shoulders slumped and she rolled her head. "I'm in no mood, Conall."

"Well, I'm not taking no for an answer. Besides, if ye're leaving in a week's time, then ye'll need to know how to make these on yer own. I can't have ye turning up on my doorstep every time ye're craving crepes."

He had to smile when she glared at him. "You wish, boyo."

By the gods, he loved everything about her. He set the bowl in front of her. "Start with the eggs. This is more of a method than a recipe, so you can make any amount ye want. For the two of us, I'd say three to four eggs should do."

She cracked the eggs in the bowl and took the whisk he handed her. "Believe it or not, I do know how to cook."

"Didn't say ye didn't. Now whisk in enough flour to thicken it. About the consistency of a very thick cake batter." He slid the bag of flour and a spoon over to her, and then dug out a chopstick.

While she added the flour, he moved behind her and slipped his hands under her hair, gathering it up to expose that gorgeous length of neck. He then twisted her hair up and pinned it in place with the chopstick, his hands trailing down her arms.

Unable to resist, he kissed that sweet spot where her neck curved into her shoulder, but his heart ached when she stiffened. "Sorry. I shouldn't have."

She sighed and her shoulders relaxed just a little. "Don't be sorry. Actually…it was nice." She looked over at him with a tentative smile before turning back to the batter. "How's this look?"

"A little more flour. That'll keep the crepes from tearing and being too delicate when we try to flip them." He grabbed the milk and tried to concentrate on cooking rather than getting his hopes up. Still… she'd said it was nice. He sighed with relief. At least it was a step in the right direction. "Now stir in enough milk to bring the mixture to the consistency of cream. Add a pinch of salt, a drop of vanilla and a spoonful or two of sugar, and ye're good to go."

Conall reached around her and grabbed a large non-stick pan and placed it on the stovetop, setting the burner to medium. When he felt her eyes on him, he threw her a smile. "Ye know, having ye around has absolutely ruined my reputation for being a cantankerous grump."

A smile tugged at her lips. "Ye're nothing but trouble, Conall Stewart. And I appreciate this—trying to distract me."

"Distract ye?" He gave her a crooked smile, his eyes full of mischief. "My dear sweet Maggie, if I was trying to distract ye from yer troubles, I could certainly think of better ways than cooking. Not that ye'd be interested."

"Ye're not going to goad me into sex, Conall." She turned to him with one eyebrow perked, and a stern gaze, like a librarian who'd caught a noisy child. "Now, are ye going to tell me how to cook these?"

"Aye, seeing that I'm in no mood for crepes thick as shoe leather. I'll do the first, and then you can have a go." He spread a pat of butter over the hot surface and then took the pan off the heat, holding it in the air. Using a ladle, he poured the batter into the pan, quickly swirling it to coat the entire surface and then returned it to the heat. After a minute or two, he removed the crepe from the pan, flipped it for a minute and then set it aside on a large plate. "I find the pan's just a wee bit hot if it's still on the stove when ye pour yer batter, and it'll keep the batter from easily coating the pan. If need be, a bit more milk can be added to thin the batter."

He stepped to the side and leaned against the counter to watch her. She repeated his steps, but the batter didn't make it all the way around. She laughed. "All right. I'll admit, ye made it look easy."

He flicked his eyebrows up with a teasing smile, happy she'd forgotten a few of her troubles, even if only for a short while. "Here. We'll do it together."

She buttered the pan and got a ladle of batter. He came up from behind her and placed his hand gently over hers, trying to ignore the way his pulse raced as their bodies brushed against each other. The moment she poured the batter, he got her swirling it around, his hand guiding hers to get the speed right. "Just keep moving it until it coats the pan evenly."

She set it back down on the heat for a few minutes more before flipping the crepe and removing it to a plate. She looked over her shoulder at him with a wide smile and then turned to face him. "How do ye like that?"

"Only because ye had an amazingly wonderful teacher, aye?" Conall laughed and then gave her a quick peck though he didn't linger, not wanting to push things. "So, is that all ye're feeding us? I'm starving, lass."

"You're such a cheeky bastard." She turned back to the crepes and got started on the next one when Conall's phone chimed.

Conall pulled his phone from his pocket and checked the text message. "It's Thorsen. The team's together and they're on for tonight. He's also coordinated with our local police to pick up Sean at the same time, so he's not tipped off. We'll have news by morning at the latest."

"Morning. And then it'll all be over, right?" Her words came out all a tumble, her breaths shallow. "He'll be home safe?"

"Aye, love." Needing to comfort her, he pulled her into his arms, his heart racing with hope when she wrapped her arms tightly around his waist. With her head resting against his shoulder, he held her close. "It's nearly over."

Though she stayed there in his arms a few moments more, it wasn't nearly enough for him. Not when she might leave him for good. She turned back to the stove, but she was still a shaky mess. "I still haven't fed ye. You must be starving."

He covered her hand with his when she grabbed the pan. "I'll take care of it, love. Why don't ye get some jams and cream out of the fridge, unless ye prefer something savory."

She stood there, her gaze finding his as she wrapped her arms around herself. "Ye're a good man, Conall."

With a crooked smile, he leaned over and gave her a peck on her cheek. "Just don't go telling anyone. That's our little secret."

Waiting to hear from Thorsen had time trickling by slower than ice melting on a day hovering just above freezing. Conall had tried to keep the conversation going, but no matter the topic, it didn't take long before

Maggie fell into silence, the worry in her eyes paining him. He needed to distract her, but didn't think she'd be up for his normal methods.

Something would need to be done, and he knew just the thing, even if it would be hard for him. Maggie had been curious about his guitar and had wanted him to play for her until she found out the reason he'd abandoned playing was because of Janet. He'd been in too dark a place back then, and though that was a long time ago, his guitar had remained in its corner, untouched.

Until now.

ONE SCENARIO AFTER the other played out in Maggie's mind, keeping her from finding any peace and dragging out the minutes so each felt like an eternity. Poor Conall. He was doing everything he could think of to keep her mind off Aidan, short of taking her to his bed. That might be the one thing to distract her sufficiently. Except for the fact that she was now the one pushing him away.

It left her questioning why, especially when she still loved him. Part of it was that her stubborn streak had kicked in. She said it'd be his final chance before she moved on, and true to her word, part of her had indeed done just that. But there was more to it.

If he was skittish and distrusting enough to not be able to get over the lies she told to keep her brother safe, then she wasn't sure she could trust him to not walk away the next time there was a bump in the road. And life was filled with bumps. No one got a smooth ride—not if they were actually living their life.

It wasn't that she didn't share in the blame. She should have been honest with him about her brother's kidnapping, even if she'd been scared to do so. Of course he would have been there for her, and would've helped support her. She knew that from the start, yet she hadn't trusted her gut. Hadn't trusted him. And he had every right to wonder if she'd lie to him again in the future.

When it came down to it, they'd both been stupid fools. Lesson learned, if a little late.

Conall reached out and gave her hand a squeeze, his eyes shadowed with an emotion she couldn't quite read. "Why don't ye get us another whisky? I think I'm going to need it."

"Sure." Her gaze lingered on him for a moment, thinking there was a nervousness in his stance and gaze. But she did as he asked without questioning him, and wandered over to where he kept his spirits.

And then she heard it, the pluck of guitar strings being tuned. The guitar he wouldn't touch, wouldn't play. He hadn't said much about it, but she knew he'd once been a different man, someone who'd been carefree enough to sing and make music. Before he'd been repeatedly hurt. Before his trust had been abused.

Her emotions rose to the surface. He knew she needed a distraction and so he was going to ignore his own wounds to heal hers. With a deep breath to steady herself, she grabbed their drinks and wandered back over to him, putting his glass down on the table near him.

"Ye don't have to, you know." By the gods, she loved him something fierce.

"I want to." He looked up from what he was doing, his eyes soft and kind as they fell on her. A crooked smile then sprung to his lips. "Not that ye'll get me to sing—unless ye're in the mood for a bit of comedy."

He strummed it experimentally and made some final adjustments. With a final bit of liquid courage, he took a long draw from his glass, set it aside, and took a deep breath.

With his head bent over the guitar, he cradled it against him like a long-lost lover returned to his arms and started to play. It was a tune of old, slow and haunting, belonging to this place, though of another time. The melody filled her like the ache of a love stolen, of a longing that would never die.

So filled with emotion, with honesty, the tune linked her heart to his. It joined their souls, for they belonged to each other and no one else.

She lost herself in the moment as he played, helpless to stop the tears that rolled down her cheeks, her throat tight. It was beautiful. So incredibly beautiful. And when he finished it was as if she was missing a part of herself.

"Och, love. I didn't mean to make ye cry." He set aside his guitar and closed the distance between. Cupping her cheek, he wiped her tears, his touch gentle as his eyes settled on hers, taking her in. "Whist, *mo chridhe*. Ye need not worry. I'm here for ye."

"I love ye, Conall." She leaned in and kissed him. Kissed him until the emptiness in her heart was filled. Kissed him until he made her whole once more.

He brushed the hair from her face, his gaze looking through to her very soul. "Marry me, Maggie. I love ye. With all that I am, I love ye and swear to do right by ye. Ye said life's too short and we should live it to its fullest, but I can't live my life without you in it." He slipped down onto one knee, sending her heart pounding. "Please, say ye'll marry me, love."

She touched his face as her eyes searched his, her breath catching as she tried to slow her racing mind. She loved him like she'd loved no other. She'd never feel whole without him in her life—not when he was her all.

With a deep breath, she took that leap of faith, knowing he'd be there to catch her. "Aye, I'll marry ye, love."

He smiled as she wrapped her arms around his neck and he kissed her. Kissed her until the rest of the world fell away around them, and there was nothing but their love.

Pulled from her stolen sleep, Maggie's heart pounded at the sound of Conall's phone ringing. He gently shifted her out of his arms and quickly moved to answer it. It was late. Nearly four in the morning. It could only be Thorsen.

He said little as he listened on the other line, grabbing her hand and giving it a squeeze. She tried not to think the worst, but was so on edge she couldn't push the thoughts out of her head. She held her breath as he hung up. "They have him, love. They've taken him to the hospital to make sure he's all right, but Thorsen said other than looking a little worse for wear, he's fine. Sean was also taken into custody and charged, and they're questioning Andrew to see if he had any part in this."

Relief overwhelmed her, the weight of worry and uncertainty finally lifting. She threw her arms around his neck and kissed him. "I can't believe it's over—and he's safe. I can't thank you enough, Conall. And Thorsen, too."

He held her close, her head resting over his heart, the beat of it steady and strong. "Together, my love. Together we can get through anything."

"Which is why we'll never part."

The lover's stone. Barely a month had passed since Conall had proposed. Maggie now stood in the heather, surrounded by ancient stones in an ancient land, their family and friends at their sides, the wind catching the white lace of her dress, the Stewart tartan draped over her shoulder. She passed her hand through the hole in the stone, linking it with Conall's, two souls, two hearts becoming one as they were married.

Conall pulled her into his arms, his eyes alight with love, with happiness, the rest of the world fading away so it was just the two of them. "I love ye, Maggie Stewart. Ye're my very breath, the blood in my veins and the very beat of my heart."

"And you, my love, are my very soul."

The End

Thorsen's story, the first book in the Mermaid Isle Series, will be available for purchase in the summer of 2013. For updates or to sign up for Cali's newsletter, please check out http://calimackay.com.

www.ingramcontent.com/pod-product-compliance
Lightning Source LLC
Chambersburg PA
CBHW050935120626
46552CB00001B/212